"I want you to know I'm here if you need a helping hand," Clint said.

Tears welled in Kristen's eyes. "I appreciate that, but I think everything's under control—except my relationship with Beatrice. I arranged to have her bedroom furniture shipped here, though, so I can re-create a familiar environment for her. Maybe that will help."

"Any pressure at work because of the emergency time off?"

"No. Day care's the big issue."

"There's a woman in town who's watched children for other people on occasion. I can give you her name, if you like."

"That would be great."

"Are you certain there's nothing else you need?"

Instead of responding in words, she closed her eyes and swayed toward him a fraction.

Without stopping to consider whether his actions were wise, Clint closed the space between them and pulled her into a hug.

She stiffened, but he didn't let her go.

Books by Irene Hannon

Love Inspired

*Home for the Holidays
*A Groom of Her Own
*A Family to Call Her Own
It Had to Be You
One Special Christmas
The Way Home
Never Say Goodbye
Crossroads
†The Best Gift
†Gift from the Heart
†The Unexpected Gift
All Our Tomorrows
The Family Man
Rainbow's End
**From This Day Forward
**A Dream to Share

**Where Love Abides
Apprentice Father
††Tides of Hope
††The Hero Next Door
††The Doctor's Perfect Match
††A Father for Zach
Child of Grace
§Seaside Reunion
§Finding Home
§Seaside Blessings

*Vows
†Sisters & Brides
**Heartland Homecoming
††Lighthouse Lane
§Starfish Bay

IRENE HANNON,

who writes both romance and romantic suspense, is the author of more than forty novels, including the bestselling Heroes of Quantico and Guardians of Justice series. Her books have been honored with two coveted RITA® Awards (the "Oscar" of romantic fiction), a National Readers' Choice Award, a Carol Award, a HOLT Medallion, a Retailers Choice Award, a Daphne du Maurier Award and two Reviewers' Choice Awards from *RT Book Reviews* magazine. *Booklist* also named one of her novels a "Top 10 Inspirational Fiction" title for 2011. A former corporate communications executive with a Fortune 500 company, Irene now writes full-time from her home in Missouri. For more information, visit www.irenehannon.com.

Seaside Blessings
Irene Hannon

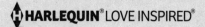

HARLEQUIN® LOVE INSPIRED®

Recycling programs
for this product may
not exist in your area.

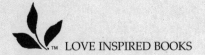 LOVE INSPIRED BOOKS

ISBN-13: 978-0-373-18932-8

SEASIDE BLESSINGS

www.LoveInspiredBooks.com

Printed in U.S.A.

Hope deferred makes the heart sick,
but a wish fulfilled is a tree of life.
—*Proverbs* 13:12

To Dorothy Hannon—
the perfect mother.

I'm so grateful you're my mom—
and my friend.

Chapter One

What had she gotten herself into?

Kristen Andrews eyed the leaden skies over the gray Pacific Ocean as she maneuvered her rental car around yet another curve on cliff-hugging Highway 101. Wasn't California supposed to be sunny and warm? Or did that description only apply to the southern part of the state?

She checked the outside temperature gauge on the dash. Forty-eight degrees on April 2. Hardly spring weather. Northern California must play by different rules—unless the cold was an aberration.

She hoped.

Otherwise, she was going to start having serious second thoughts about trading in the tropical warmth of Maui for Starfish Bay.

Cranking the heater up another notch, she checked the map on the seat beside her. Less than five miles to go. Maybe her new home would make up in charm what it lacked in warmth.

But ten minutes later, as she took inventory of the five-block-long stretch of 101 that comprised Starfish Bay's straggling main street, her spirits sank. A biker bar and the cheesy-looking Orchid Café and Motel bookended assorted shops and small businesses, including a general mercantile store, post office and dentist. An art gallery was the only bright spot. If she didn't have to spend the next few nights at the motel, she'd get a good laugh out of the gaudy sign in front that featured a huge purple orchid.

She was in no mood for mirth, however.

What in the world had the president of Mattson Properties seen in this place to merit spending millions of dollars on an upscale destination resort?

But a few minutes later, she had her answer. After pulling into the resort entrance and following a winding road through a spruce and hemlock forest, she emerged onto a windswept headland that soared above the ocean.

Wow.

The view alone would bring people in.

In the far distance, a slight haze softened the line where sea and sky met. To the right and left, other headlands jutted into the blue water along the irregular coast, their steeply sloping rock faces sporting forested or barren tops, some of them wrapped in horizontal tendrils of cloud. Offshore from the tiny beaches and cliff bases, jagged boulders thrust through the surface of the water, aiming for the sky as the surf churned around them.

The resort was none too shabby, either. Not that she'd expected it to be. Louis Mattson didn't do things on the cheap. The low-slung two-story structure, constructed of wood and stone and huge expanses of glass, hugged the sloping headland, blending perfectly into the landscape and reeking of understated elegance.

Her anxiety dissipated a smidgen. It didn't have palm trees or tropical breezes, but Inn at The Point would be a pleasant place to work until she was asked to move on again. And when that time came, she'd leave with no regrets—and no strings. Like always.

A sudden pang of melancholy tugged at her heart, and she tightened her grip on the wheel.

Focus on the future, Kristen, not the past. Once you get settled in here, your mood will improve. It always does.

Fortified by her little pep talk, she followed the curving drive that led to the main entrance. The front door opened to disgorge some of the construction workers, and she stopped to let them pass. Painters, judging by their white pants and shirts. Too bad the place wouldn't be ready for occupancy for another month. She'd much rather spend the next few nights here than at the Orchid Motel. But at least she'd get a tour tomorrow, when she met with Mark Stephens, the general manager.

In the meantime, she might as well check in at the motel. And maybe she could find a slicker at the Mercantile. Given the ominous sky, chilly temperature and puddles of water on the inn's drive, she was going to need one.

She rounded the circle drive and accelerated back toward 101, groping in her purse for her lipstick. After her dash through the rain to the rental car at the Arcata/Eureka airport, she could imagine the state of her makeup. The repairs she'd made in San Francisco between plane changes had probably been washed away long ago.

Keeping one hand on the wheel, she set the lipstick in her lap, adjusted the rearview mirror and checked out her appearance. Not great. The shadows under her eyes from the long trans-Pacific flight made her look older than her thirty-one years, and her blush and lipstick had faded. A quick touch-up before…

"Hey! Watch it!"

The muffled shout jerked her attention back to the road. Somehow she'd drifted toward the shoulder—and in another two seconds she was going to sideswipe a compact pickup truck that hadn't been there when she'd arrived.

Heart hammering, she wrenched the wheel to the left…and sent a spray of water from a puddle all over the guy who'd yelled at her.

Once clear of the truck, she jammed on the brakes, closed her eyes and took a slow, deep breath. Then another. Whew. That had been a close…

A loud tap sounded on her window, a few inches from her ear, and she jerked again.

Clenching the wheel, she turned her head to find a tall, broad-shouldered man with dark brown hair, piercing blue eyes and an angry glare giving her the evil eye. Fresh mud was splattered across his sweatshirt and jeans.

What she noticed most, though, was the ax in his hands. A big ax. Like the kind in the stories about Paul Bunyan.

When she remained frozen, he motioned for her to roll down her window.

Double-checking that her car doors were locked, she pried her fingers off the wheel and cracked the window two inches.

"Sorry about that." Her apology came out shaky.

His gaze flicked to the lipstick in her lap and he narrowed his eyes. "In the future, I'd suggest you focus on your driving instead of your appearance."

Warmth stole onto her cheeks, and irritation steadied—and sharpened— her voice. "You don't have to be rude about it. I said I was sorry."

Instead of responding, he gave her a once-over. Not the appreciative kind she was accustomed to from men, but one fraught with disapproval.

"This is private property. Didn't you see the sign at the entrance?"

Her hackles rose. Who was this guy to question her? He didn't look as if he belonged here, either. He wasn't even close to the main job site, and his casual, rugged clothing didn't match the white attire of the painters she'd seen coming out the front door.

"I happen to work for Mattson Properties. And you are?"

He gave her another appraising perusal. "You're not a construction worker, and the only staff on-site so far is Mark Stephens."

Okay, so he knew the manager's name. Maybe he was legit. "I'm the concierge."

One side of his mouth quirked up in a humorless smile. "I can buy that. You look the type."

She had no idea what that was supposed to mean—but his tone wasn't positive. "You never told me who you were."

As drops of rain began leaving dark splotches on his denim shirt, he scanned the sky and hoisted the ax over his shoulder. "Mark knows I'm here. So does Mattson. And put the lipstick away before you venture onto 101. The highway curves are a lot less forgiving."

With that, he turned and marched toward the woods.

Fingers still trembling, Kristen watched him in the rearview mirror as she put the car back in gear. He hadn't told her who he was.

But that was fine.

Because if she was lucky, their paths would never cross again.

"Yes. Here it is. Kristen Andrews for three nights." The white-haired woman touched an entry in the handwritten reservation book. "Welcome to the Orchid Café and Motel. I'm Genevieve Durham." Smiling across the eat-in counter that also served as a front desk for the adjacent motel, she extended her hand. "I hope you'll have a pleasant stay."

Kristen's fingers were engulfed in a firm

clasp and given a vigorous shake as she responded. "Thank you."

The woman tapped a line on the registration form for Kristen to sign. "You don't look like our typical guest. My sister Lillian and I have owned this place for more than a dozen years, and most visitors are either fishermen or redwood gawkers. I don't peg you as either."

"You're right. I'm not. I work for Mattson Properties." She completed her signature and handed the woman's pen back. "I'm the concierge and event planner for the inn."

"Ah. Our competition."

Hardly. But Kristen opted for diplomacy instead. "I expect we may be catering to a different clientele."

"True." The woman's eyes sparkled with mirth. "You all will get the rich folks—and that's just fine. Long as they spend some of their money in town." She tucked the registration slip into the reservation book and stowed the bulging volume under the counter. "So where will you be living? Starfish Bay could use some new blood."

"I haven't decided yet. The commute from Eureka or Crescent City doesn't appeal to me, but it depends on what's available here. I jotted down a few numbers from the bulletin board at the Mercantile when I stopped in for this." She gestured to the yellow, hooded slicker she'd purchased.

"I'm sure you'll find a nice spot here. The fog can make driving tricky, so it would be better to live close. How would you like to pay the deposit for the room?"

Kristen dug through her purse and handed over her credit card, watching in amusement as the woman fitted it into one of those old-fashioned machines that required manually pushing a lever over the plastic rectangle to get an impression of the numbers. No surprise, though, given the ancient cash register beside it.

The woman handed the card back. "The dining room is just opening for dinner, if you'd care to stay. We have pot roast tonight—a house specialty—and my sister made blackberry cobbler. I don't mean to brag, but we have regular customers who drive all the way from Eureka and Crescent City for our home cooking."

Kristen hesitated. The aromas wafting from the kitchen pass-through behind the counter were setting off a rumble in her stomach, and lunch had been a long time ago. If the food tasted half as delicious as it smelled, she'd at least eat well while she was here.

"I think I will."

"Wonderful." Genevieve beamed at her and picked up a menu. "I have a nice cozy table by the window."

Once she was seated, Kristen ordered, checked her voice mail and responded to a few emails, jotting notes on the orchid-festooned paper place mat that proclaimed, "Wish upon a star in Starfish Bay—where dreams come true."

She shook her head at the flowery adage. Sentimental poppycock like that could lead to trouble—as could romanticized dreams of living happily ever after. She'd learned that the hard way.

But the past was the past, and she refused to dwell on it.

By the time Genevieve delivered a heaping plate of pot roast with savory potatoes and carrots, she'd shifted gears and was perusing the phone numbers and addresses of rental units she'd jotted down at the Mercantile.

The woman deposited the plate in front of her, then peered over her shoulder at the notebook resting on the table.

"That one's your best bet." She tapped the second address. "Nice, quiet location. Well kept. Wonderful landlord. Very warm and welcoming. It would be perfect for you. I'd be happy to give you directions."

"Could I impose on you for directions to all three?"

"Of course. It won't take but a minute. Everything's easy to find in Starfish Bay. Ready?"

Kristen picked up her pen and wrote the instructions as the woman dictated.

"But I'd start with that one, if I were you." Once again, Genevieve tapped the second address.

"I'll do that." Kristen tucked the notebook in her purse and dug into the pot roast.

Twenty minutes later, as she was finishing off the last bite of blackberry cobbler, the café owner returned and gave her clean plate an approving nod. "You did real fine."

Kristen dabbed at her lips with the napkin and shot the woman a rueful look as she stood. "Too many meals like that, and I'll have to buy a new wardrobe."

The older woman gave her attire an admiring sweep. "Speaking of wardrobes— that's a mighty pretty outfit. Reminds me of the cruise Lillian and I took in Hawaii fifteen years ago."

Kristen glanced at her beige capris and green silk blouse with a subtle hibiscus pattern. "As a matter of fact, it's from Hawaii. That's where I've been working for the past three years. But it's not too practical for this climate." She slipped her arms into the yellow slicker as she spoke.

"It is a mite cooler here. Lillian and I are from Georgia, so we were used to a bit more heat, too. But you can't beat this scenery." She picked up Kristen's empty plate. "You let me know if there's anything you need in your room."

"I will. And thanks for a great dinner." With a lift of her hand, she headed for the door.

Twenty minutes later, as the shadows began to lengthen, Kristen had to admit Genevieve had been right on all scores. The home cooking at the Orchid was fabulous, all of the rental properties had been easy to find and the second one on the list was by far the nicest.

She pulled to a stop in front of the two-story, two-family unit she'd circled back to after driving past all three.

Constructed of natural wood stained a golden/reddish color, it featured a cantilevered balcony across the whole second floor, above the front door. The wood of the railing matched the house, as did the stairway on the side that led to the balcony and a side entry on the upper level. A stone walk wound to the front door, which had flower boxes on either side. The property appeared to be in meticulous condition.

And the price was right.

She reread the notes she'd jotted at the Mercantile. The ad had said it was available for showing after six, and it was ten past. As long as she was here, why not drop in? That might be better than calling ahead. Seeing a place on the spur of the moment, in its unprimped state, often worked to a renter's advantage, as she'd discovered over the past nine years.

Tucking the slicker around her, she picked up her purse and slid out of the rental car. A fine mist hung in the air, and she hurried toward the front door, admiring the half circle of paned glass at the top and the long panels of art glass on each side. But the wind had picked up, and once under the balcony she wasted no time pressing the bell.

If nothing else, a tour of the apartment would get her out of the chill. And if the landlord was as warm and welcoming as Genevieve had promised, perhaps she'd even be offered a comforting cup of tea.

Finger-combing his wet hair, Clint Nolan padded barefoot toward the front of the house as the doorbell gave a second, impatient peal. After spending the past hour fighting a stubborn tree root on the nature trail at The Point, he wanted food, not visitors. And he didn't intend to devote a lot of time to this one. Dinner had already been delayed, thanks to the shower—a necessity after the muddy dousing the inn's concierge had given him.

His blood pressure inched up a notch. Talk about unpleasant encounters.

Forcibly changing his scowl to the semblance of a smile, he unlocked the door, pulled it open—and froze.

It was her.

Miss Lipstick-Wielding Reckless Driver.

And she didn't look any too happy to

see the ax-wielding victim of her splash attack, either.

His smile morphed back to a scowl.

At least she'd had the common sense to cover her out-of-place tropical-looking clothing with a practical yellow slicker.

But she couldn't change her appearance. Same vivid jade-colored eyes. Same shoulder-length strawberry-blond hair. Same lush lashes. Same classic oval face.

Same uncanny—and unsettling—resemblance to Lisa.

Several seconds of silence ticked by.

When she didn't seem inclined—or able—to take the initiative, he finally spoke. "Can I help you?" The question came out cool and clipped.

"Um…" She fiddled with the strap of her purse, staring at his T-shirt.

He glanced down, wondering which one he'd grabbed out of the drawer. Oh, yeah. The one with the skull and crossbones that said, "Jaz's World-Famous Biker Bar."

His lips flexed. No wonder Miss High-

End Concierge was staring. Biker bars would *not* be her thing.

She cleared her throat. "I, uh, got your address from the rentals section of the Mercantile's bulletin board. Genevieve at the Orchid recommended your place when I, uh, ate dinner there."

The glitch in her composure didn't surprise him. Neither did the referral. Since he'd arrived in town almost three years ago, the sisters at the Orchid had been lamenting over his single state. Especially Genevieve.

But the Orchid Café matchmaker was wasting her time in this case. The inn's concierge wasn't the woman for him. No way. No how.

And the concierge herself seemed to agree. She looked as if she couldn't wait to extract herself from this awkward situation and beat a hasty retreat.

He'd make it easy for her.

"I doubt you'd be interested. It's on the rustic side."

A spark of indignation sprang to life in

the depths of those green irises, and her chin lifted in a defiant tilt.

Uh-oh. Wrong move.

"Depends on what you mean by *rustic*. Are you telling me it doesn't have indoor plumbing?"

Cute.

He folded his arms across his chest, giving her a few grudging points for the quick comeback. "It has a full bath and a compact kitchen. Very compact."

"How many bedrooms?"

"Two. Plus living room and breakfast nook."

"It's furnished, correct?"

"With the basics."

"I'd like to see it."

Okay. She'd called his bluff. This woman was no airhead, even if she did spend her days arranging cushy excursions and making dinner reservations for rich hotel guests. There was an undeniable spark of intelligence—and spunk—in her eyes. She might be uncomfortable around him, she might know he didn't want her as a tenant, but she hadn't liked the implication of his rustic comment one little bit and she was going to make him pay for it.

Clint debated his options. He could tell her the place had already been rented and send her on her way—but she'd find out the truth eventually.

Besides, he didn't lie.

Dinner would have to wait a few more minutes.

"Fine." He gestured to the stairs on the side of the house. "I'll meet you up there."

He closed the door in her face.

Hoping she'd leave.

Knowing she wouldn't.

Thoroughly aggravated, he started toward the kitchen to retrieve the key. Halfway there, he stopped, planted his fists on his hips and frowned.

Why was he so irritated, anyway?

Yes, the woman had doused him on The Point. Yes, her inattentive driving had annoyed him. But she hadn't sideswiped his car, and he'd been doused and muddied by nature plenty of times.

That left only one explanation for his bad mood.

Her resemblance to Lisa.

And that was completely irrational. The new concierge wasn't his ex-fiancée. She didn't have a thing to do with all the bad memories he'd come out here to forget. Conclusion? His rudeness was out of line.

Heaving a sigh, he continued to the kitchen, retrieved the keys from a hook, shoved his feet into a pair of deck shoes and exited through the back door. Okay. He'd be polite, answer her questions—and wait for her to leave. And she *would* leave. She was only putting him through these paces as a payback for his snotty remark.

He found her waiting on the landing at the top of the steps. In silence, he fitted the key into the lock, pushed the door open and gestured her inside.

After wiping her damp shoes on the mat inside the door, she did a slow circuit of the place, lingering by the sliding glass doors in the living room that led to the balcony and offered a glimpse of the sea in the distance. He stayed in the galley kitchen while she inspected the place, the open floor plan allowing him to keep her in sight until she disappeared down the hall. Sixty seconds later, he heard a toilet flush.

She was checking out the indoor plumbing.

A smile twitched at his lips, which he stifled at once.

He was not going to be amused by her antics.

When she reappeared, she crossed the living room and stopped a few feet away in the dinette area.

"How long has this been vacant?" She regarded him across the stool-lined countertop that separated them.

"Six weeks. The older couple who rented it had some health issues, so they moved into assisted living in Eureka. The furnishings are the things they left behind."

"And you live below?"

"Yes."

She tightened her grip on her purse.

"Since we've never been formally introduced..." She closed the distance between them and extended her hand. "Kristen Andrews."

Left with no choice, he took her slender fingers in his, surprised by her firm grip. "Clint Nolan."

"Thanks for the tour. I'll think about it and call you." She sashayed toward the door.

Flummoxed, he stared after her. What had happened to the "thanks but no thanks" he'd expected?

Feeling as if he was losing control of the situation, he intercepted her at the door. "It's not that easy. I'll need to check your credit rating and your references."

She paused and angled toward him, close enough now for him to see the faint sprinkling of freckles across her nose. To catch a whiff of some subtle, no doubt expensive, scent. And to note the slight, condescending arch of her eyebrows. The cool, composed concierge was back.

"If I decide I'm interested, I'll pass your

credit and character check with flying colors. Mr. Mattson himself will vouch for me. I've been in his employ for nine years. Good night, Mr. Nolan."

Turning, she exited onto the landing and disappeared down the steps.

Clint stood unmoving for a couple of minutes, hand grasped around the edge of the door as he fought down a ridiculous flutter of panic. What was wrong with him, anyway? He didn't have to rent to her. The final decision was his, not hers. If she even contacted him again.

And that was a big *if,* despite her glib parting commentary. Given their rocky start, why would she want to live under the same roof with him? There were plenty of other places to rent, even if they weren't as nice as his. He'd sweated blood renovating this place as he worked through his anger and grief. But the other properties were adequate.

Feeling calmer, he exited onto the landing. At the intersection in the distance, he caught a glimpse of taillights through the trees. Then the midsize rental car pulled out and disappeared from his street.

Just as he hoped its driver would disappear from his life.

Chapter Two

The jarring jangle of the windup alarm clock yanked Kristen out of a sound sleep in the early-morning dimness, and she groped for the instrument of torture on the nightstand.

Her fingers encountered a smooth, cylindrical object. That would be…the vase containing a spray of silk orchids. She tried again. The instant she located the clock, she smashed down the button to shut off the offending noise.

In the blessed silence that followed, Kristen sank back onto the pillow and pulled the covers up to her chin, giving her pulse a minute to return to normal after the rude reveille. Too bad the Orchid Motel didn't provide luxuries like musical wake-up calls instead of old-fashioned alarm clocks. Inn at The Point guests would be coaxed out of their sound sleep much more gently.

On the other hand, they wouldn't snuggle under handmade quilts or find homemade cinnamon rolls in their room. Kristen eyed the half-consumed confection on the small table next to the easy chair by the window. She'd found it last night, along with a sweet note from Genevieve, when she'd returned from a full day interviewing applicants for the part-time assistant concierge positions and buying a new car in Eureka. The rest of the roll would make a more-than-satisfactory breakfast before she hit the road for the drive south to catch her return flight to Hawaii.

Focused on the treat, she threw back the covers, swung her feet to the floor and padded over to the table. As she broke off a bite and popped it into her mouth, she moved aside the curtains with her free hand to see if by chance the rain and gray skies that had persisted during her visit had cleared.

"What in the world...?"

She stopped chewing and peered into the obfuscating grayness.

Was that fog?

Yes. A thick blanket of it. She couldn't even see her car, and it was parked less than a dozen feet away.

So how was she supposed to get to the airport?

Tamping down her panic, she dispensed with her usual shower, threw on her clothes and tossed all her belongings into her suitcase to be sorted through later. After running a brush through her hair and applying the bare minimum of makeup, she stepped outside and felt her way along the wall toward the café. Hoping for...a miracle? Maybe. Given the nonexistent visibility, that was what it might take to get her to the airport in time for her plane.

Despite the dismal weather, a few Saturday-morning diners had braved the elements and were enjoying their morning meal in the café when Kristen pushed through the door.

"My, you're up bright and early for a weekend." Genevieve picked up a menu and gave her a smile that was far sunnier than the weather. "We're making pecan waffles, if you're in the mood for a hearty breakfast."

Kristen crossed to the counter. "Not today, thanks. Just coffee, to go. And I need to settle my bill. I've got a plane to catch—if I can get out of here in this fog."

"No worries." The woman set the menu aside and pulled the bulging reservation book from beneath the counter. "It'll lift in less than an hour."

Kristen gave the fog a dubious perusal over her shoulder. "How do you know?"

"I've lived here a fair number of years. You learn to read the weather. Morning fog doesn't usually linger past nine. Afternoon fog…that's a different story. It can last all night, and it plays havoc with the commuters." Genevieve tallied up the bill and ran the credit card Kristen offered her, handing over the slip for a signature. "Did you decide on a place to live?"

Until ten minutes ago, Kristen would have said yes. After spending an afternoon with a real estate agent in Eureka, she'd more or less settled on a pleasant condo. It might not be as nice—or convenient—as Clint's place, but it was a whole lot more neutral.

Now, thanks to the fog, her resolve wavered.

"I'm still mulling over my options." She slipped the credit card back into her wallet and slung the strap of the purse over her shoulder. "But I'm leaning toward one of the places I visited."

Genevieve poured her coffee into a to-go cup, pressed on a plastic lid and handed it over. "In town?"

"No. Eureka."

"Clint's place didn't pass muster?"

She transferred her weight from one foot to the other and took a sip of the caffeine-laced brew. "It was very nice."

"I thought you'd like it. And you couldn't

find a better landlord. He's handy with tools, so you'd never have to worry about maintenance issues. Not that you're likely to have any. He refurbished that place top to bottom after he moved here three years ago. I know the Clarks—his previous tenants—hated to leave. Clint often picked up prescriptions for them, or came here to get them take-out dinners after Ella's health started to fail."

Kristen caught her lower lip between her teeth. Were they talking about the same guy?

Maybe.

When she'd mentioned her unsettling encounter with him to Mark Stephens, the inn's general manager had also sung his praises. He'd told her Clint had done a lot of the grunt work for the Save the Point campaign that Lindsey at the Mercantile had organized to try to block development of the headland. And it seemed her ax-toting stranger had not only found a firm to develop an interpretive trail through the buffer zone between 101 and the resort—which Mattson had set aside as a public nature preserve—but had taken on a lot of the trail-clearing work himself on his days off.

Kristen took another look out the window. In light of the fickle fog, living five versus fifty minutes from work held a lot of appeal. "I haven't ruled out his place."

"Glad to hear it." The door opened to admit more customers, and once more Genevieve picked up some menus. "When will you be back to stay?"

"Two weeks. I have to wrap up some transition details in Hawaii before Inn at The Point opens."

"Well, you have a safe trip home. Are you sure you don't have time for breakfast?"

"No. Besides, I'm still working on that fabulous cinnamon roll you left me last night. Thank you for that. It was a nice surprise after a very long day."

The café owner patted her hand en route to welcome the new diners. "A pleasure, my dear. Starfish Bay people take care of their friends."

As the woman bustled off toward the dining room, a young couple in tow, Kristen crossed the small foyer and exited into the fog. Was it a bit less dense now—or was that only wishful thinking? She squinted. No, she could see the outline of her car in the distance. Genevieve had been right. The pea soup was dissipating.

And perhaps she was right about Clint's apartment, too. It *was* convenient, and the man did sound like an excellent landlord. Plus, it wasn't as if she had to socialize with him. Surely they could be civil to each other if they happened to meet in the driveway on occasion.

Besides, much to her surprise, she found herself wanting to be part of this tiny community. Clint aside, everyone else she'd met had done their best to make her feel welcome. Lindsey and her father in the Mercantile. Genevieve and Lillian. Janice, who owned the art gallery. And even though she'd taken care of herself for a long time, the notion of people taking care of their friends appealed to her, too.

Fitting the key into the door of her room, she made up her mind.

If the place was still available, and if Clint was willing to rent to her—a far bigger if—she was going to live in Starfish Bay.

Clint flipped a second pancake with one hand and sipped his coffee with the other, a smile tugging at his lips. A lazy Saturday morning was one of life's nicest pleasures. And during the off-season, he had most of them to himself. Maybe after breakfast he'd stroll down to Agate Beach and…

The sudden ring of his cell phone interrupted the pleasant strains of Vivaldi that filled his kitchen, and he picked it up from the counter, scanning the unfamiliar area code. Could be a phone solicitor. If so, he'd dispense with the annoyance quickly and get back to important stuff—like breakfast.

Punching the on button, he greeted the

caller as he slid the spatula under his third pancake and turned it over.

"Mr. Nolan? Kristen Andrews. I looked at your apartment earlier in the week."

Blood pressure spiking, he froze and stared at the small ceramic plaque hanging on the wall next to the stove that was emblazoned with words from Ephesians: "Be kind to one another, compassionate, forgiving one another as God has forgiven you in Christ."

Clenching his fist, he sucked in a breath. *Be a Christian, Nolan—even if it kills you.*

"Yes. I remember." Despite the biblical admonition inches from his face, the words came out cautious and cool.

"I'd like to rent it. I'll be happy to provide any credit or personal references you need."

What was left of his relaxed, upbeat mood evaporated. What was he supposed to do now? If she'd worked for Mattson for nine years, she no doubt had stellar references. But what other excuse could he conjure up not to rent to her?

"Mr. Nolan? Are you there?"

Yeah. Unfortunately.

He read the plaque again, shoved his fingers through his hair and paced over to the back door. The spruce trees lining his property were beginning to emerge from the fog, and a ray of sun was trying to penetrate the grayness. Through the mist he caught a glimpse of blue sky.

It might turn out to be a nice day, after all—weather-wise.

Expelling a frustrated breath, he propped a hand on his hip. "A reference check won't be necessary."

A couple of beats of silence ticked by.

"Does that mean I can rent your place?"

Did it? Could he handle having a Lisa lookalike living in such close proximity?

He wasn't sure. And he didn't want to make a decision on the spur of the moment that he might later regret.

"Look…you caught me in the middle of

something. Is there a number where I can call you later?"

"I'll be on a plane all day, on my way back to Maui. But since I'll be back in two weeks, I need to finalize my living arrangements as soon as possible." She paused, and he heard her exhale. "I realize we didn't start off on the best terms, but I can promise you I'll be an excellent tenant. I don't smoke, drink or throw wild parties. I like things clean and orderly. You won't even see much of me. I work long hours. When I do have free time, my favorite indoor pastime is reading. As a bonus, I've been known to bake my famous ginger cookies for nice neighbors. In time, you might qualify."

One side of Clint's mouth hitched up a fraction at the wry caveat. The lady had a sense of humor. "Is that a bribe?"

"Depends. Did it work?"

"Maybe." At the sound of a horn in the background, he frowned. "What was that?"

"Someone must think I'm going too slowly."

Closing his eyes, he suppressed a shudder. Who wouldn't, after witnessing her steering skills when she was distracted? "You're driving the hairpins on 101 in the fog and trying to talk on the phone at the same time?"

"I won't be if you agree to rent me the apartment."

"Okay. Fine. It's yours. Call me when you're not on the road and we'll work out the details."

"I'll do that. Thanks." The line went dead fast, as if she was afraid he'd change his mind.

Smart move. He was already having second thoughts.

But it was too late for that now. He was stuck—assuming Kristen Andrews made it to the airport in one piece.

Heaving a sigh, Clint walked back to the counter and set the phone down. He picked up the spatula, checked the bottom of his pancakes and grimaced.

While he'd talked to his new tenant, they'd gotten burned.

He hoped that wasn't an omen.

* * *

From the threshold of her front door, Kristen took one last survey of the furnished condo on Maui she'd called home for the past three years. She'd already shipped seven boxes of personal possessions to Starfish Bay. Two boxes of tropical clothing that would be out of place in redwood country had been donated to a resell shop run by a local charity. The rest of her clothes were packed in the suitcases the cabdriver was loading in the trunk.

She'd also sold her sporty little convertible, said goodbye to her coworkers and given away the plant she'd rescued from the Dumpster and resuscitated soon after her arrival.

She was ready to move on.

Kristen completed her sweep of the condo. There was nothing in this place, with its generic contemporary furnishings, to suggest she'd ever lived here. No nail holes in the walls where she'd hung family pictures. No magnets on the refrigerator that had held snapshots or a child's crude drawings. No little-girl fairy-tale-princess wallpaper border in the empty spare room.

A sudden film of moisture blurred her vision as her cell began to ring. Grateful for the interruption, she blinked a few times to bring the world back into focus, then snagged the phone out of her purse and pressed the talk button.

"Ms. Andrews? Clint Nolan. Did I catch you at a bad time?"

"No." *Liar, liar, pants on fire.* Ignoring that taunt, she stepped out and closed the door behind her without a backward look. "I'm getting ready to leave for the airport. I have a minute."

"I wanted to let you know that seven boxes of your things arrived today, but that's all that's shown up. I didn't want you to get here and find out most of your stuff never left Hawaii—or that it's halfway between here and there on a container ship."

"I appreciate the call, but that's everything I sent."

In the silence that followed, she could imagine her new landlord wrinkling his brow as he tried to figure out why she had so few personal possessions after nine years of living on her own. But she waited him out. No way did she intend to offer any explanations.

"I, uh, thought you were sending furniture."

"The apartment has everything I need for now." She tacked on the last two words as an afterthought, hoping it would appease him. In truth, the sparse furnishings were adequate for her needs. A couch, a dinette table, a bed. It was easier to leave a place behind if you didn't make it your own.

"Okay." His tone was cautious and more than a little puzzled. "If I'm not home when you get here, I'll leave the key under the mat by your door."

"That will be fine. Thanks." The cab-driver closed the trunk and rounded the car to stand by the back door. "My driver's ready to leave. I'll see you soon."

"All right. Safe journey."

A hum on the line told her he'd hung up. Dropping the phone back into her purse,

Kristen started down the walk. But as she passed a glossy-leafed bush laden with fragrant magenta plumeria, she stopped to take a whiff, as she always did. The sweet, tropical smell soothed her, reminding her that even less-than-perfect lives could hold small joys.

And as she continued toward the cab, she wondered what small joys might await her in Starfish Bay.

Chapter Three

As Kristen pulled up the dark drive that led to Clint's house, moving slowly in the brand-new Accord she'd picked up from the dealer in Eureka, she tried to remember the last time she'd been so tired. Maybe six years ago, when she'd had the flu.

At least a long, hot shower and a deep, restoring sleep were in her immediate future—as soon as she unloaded her car, stowed the groceries she'd purchased in Arcata and fixed herself a simple meal. Scrambled eggs would have to do tonight.

Slowing to a stop, she set the brake and surveyed the first floor. Lights burned on either side of the front door, but the rest of the downstairs was dark. Clint must be out. On a date, perhaps? And why not? He might not be the friendliest guy around, but he did fit the classic tall, dark and handsome profile—and that faint Southern accent only added to his appeal. A man like that wouldn't have to spend any Saturday evening alone unless he chose to.

Still, for some strange reason she'd sort of hoped he'd be around to welcome her.

How dumb was that?

Irritated by a silly sense of letdown, Kristen pulled the trunk release, pushed the door open with her shoulder and grabbed her purse. She was just jet-lagged, that was all. A solid night's sleep would restore her perspective.

Circling around to the back of the car, she sized up the sturdy wooden steps, illuminated by a light over her door, that led to the second floor. Sixty seconds later, as she lugged her first suitcase up, she again wished her landlord had been around to welcome her—for practical reasons this time. Her luggage weighed a ton, and with those bulging biceps she'd noted below the sleeves of his biker T-shirt the day she'd toured the place he could have toted her bags up without breaking a sweat.

As it was, she was huffing by the time she dumped the fourth and final bag inside the door.

For someone who'd taken full benefit of the perk that gave her unlimited access to the exercise equipment at Mattson Properties' inns, her labored panting was pathetic. That was what happened when you slacked off on a fitness regime, though. But the longer-than-usual hours she'd put in over the past couple of weeks to ensure a smooth transition at the Maui property hadn't left time for personal pursuits of any kind.

Exercise suddenly vaulted to the top of tomorrow's priority list.

She descended the steps once more to retrieve the two bags of groceries. Back at the top, she nudged the door open again with her hip and walked over to the kitchen counter, where she deposited them with a thud.

That was when she spotted the note—and the luscious-looking turkey sandwich on whole-wheat bread it was propped against. A bag of chips and two large oatmeal cookies rounded out the picture.

Her stomach growled as she approached what she hoped wasn't a mirage, picked up the small sheet of paper and scanned the three scribbled lines.

"Sorry I wasn't here to welcome you. I thought you might be tired and hungry after your trip. If not, the sandwich will keep in the fridge. See you tomorrow."

Clint had signed it in a scrawling hand.

Kristen touched the plate. Her new landlord might not be here in person to greet her, but he'd left a thoughtful token of welcome.

Nice.

Her sense of letdown faded as her spirits took a distinct uptick.

Maybe people in Starfish Bay really did take care of their friends, as Genevieve had told her. Not that she and Clint were friends. But she already knew he'd gone above and beyond with his previous tenants. She just hadn't been sure his kindness to the Clarks would extend to her.

Detouring through the living room to freshen up in the bath before she devoured his offering, she discovered he'd also lugged up her seven boxes of personal items. They were lined up behind the couch that faced the sliding glass doors, a pathetic reminder of how little she had to show for the past nine years.

As she continued toward the hall, the quixotic sentiment from the Orchid Café place mats echoed in her mind. At the time, she'd dismissed the whole notion of dreams coming true in Starfish Bay. Fairy tales belonged in storybooks, not real life.

But as she returned to the kitchen—and to the simple meal Clint had left for her— she felt more…hopeful…than she had in years. Maybe because no previous landlord had ever left her a welcome gift. Of course, in the past she'd rented through companies, never directly from an owner. The process had been businesslike and impersonal: submit to a credit and reference check, pay the first and last month's rent, provide a deposit against damages, sign a contract.

Funny. She'd done none of those things with Clint. He'd simply promised her the apartment was hers, said they'd take care of any paperwork after she arrived...and she'd believed him. Despite her dot-every-*i*-cross-every-*t* personality, it had never occurred to her to doubt his word.

Because Clint Nolan had struck her as an honorable kind of guy.

And Starfish Bay had struck her as a town where people did, indeed, take care of their friends.

In some ways, that was refreshing—and uplifting.

But there was a danger, too. She could get sucked in. Fall under the spell of the town...and the man. Put down roots.

And she couldn't let that happen.

For even if Starfish Bay could, by chance,

make dreams come true, she'd long ago given up any right to a happy ending.

Clint settled his sport coat on his shoulders, grabbed his keys, started for the front door—then stopped when he heard muffled footsteps overhead.

His tenant was up.

He'd arrived home too late last night to welcome her in person, and a quick glance at his watch told him he was already cutting it close this morning. But he could spare half a minute to say hello.

Taking the outside steps two at a time, he knocked. When there was no response after fifteen seconds, he tried again. Still nothing. Maybe she was in the shower— or disinclined to greet visitors first thing in the morning. Whatever. At least he'd tried. He'd catch her later.

But as he prepared to descend the stairs, he heard the lock being flipped. A moment later the door was pulled open.

Clint opened his mouth to say hello...but

the words died in his throat as he stared at the woman across from him.

Every other time he'd seen Kristen, her strawberry-blond tresses had been perfectly coiffed and she'd been wearing designer-type attire. Today, her hair was pulled back with some kind of scrunchy thing, highlighting her classic features. A formfitting lime-green tank top and skinny leggings that hit her midcalf showed off her curves to perfection. And the hot-pink polish on her pedicured toes was…hot.

Wow.

"Good morning."

Checking to make sure his tongue wasn't hanging out, he lifted his head at her amused greeting. Took a step back. Ran into the railing behind him on the small landing.

"Hi." His voice cracked, and he cleared his throat as warmth crept up his neck. *Get a grip, Nolan. You're not some teenager with raging adolescent hormones.* "I just wanted to welcome you in person and see if everything is okay with the apartment."

Her indulgent smile told him she knew exactly the effect she was having on him. Despite his valiant effort, the warmth crept higher and spilled onto his cheeks.

What was going on?

He hadn't had a reaction like this since Mary Lou Marconi had given him a box of chocolate hearts on Valentine's Day in third grade—in front of all his buddies.

"Everything's fine, thanks. I've even set up my yoga mat to take advantage of the great view." She moved aside to gesture toward the picture window, and he caught a glimpse of the edge of a mat in front of the couch. That explained her attire—if not his reaction. "And thank you for the sandwich and snacks. They hit the spot. I was starving when I arrived. Let me return the plate."

"That's okay. I'll get it later. I'm already running late for the Sunday service." She stopped and swiveled back toward him as he eased toward the steps. "By the way, if you need any information about area churches after you settle in, let me know."

The lingering amusement in her demeanor vanished. "Thanks for the offer, but I'm not a churchgoer."

Clint searched her eyes. He'd run into his share of nonbelievers. Some were indifferent. Some were virulently anti-Christian. Some were disappointed in God. Others were angry at the Almighty. But Kristen didn't exhibit any of those emotions. She just seemed...sad.

Why?

When she said nothing else, he took the hint and crossed the small landing toward the steps. "Well, if you need anything at any time, don't hesitate to call my cell or knock on my door. Otherwise, I won't infringe on your privacy."

"All right. Thanks."

As he continued down the stairs, he heard the soft click of the door behind him.

Once behind the wheel, he backed out and pointed the truck toward 101. But before he lost sight of his house, he glanced up at the second floor. For a fleeting instant he thought he saw Kristen in the picture window watching him.

The image melted into the shadows so quickly, however, he wondered if he'd imagined it.

He hadn't imagined that sad look in her eyes, though. Nor the meager handful of boxes containing her possessions that he'd lugged upstairs.

It didn't make sense.

She was a beautiful woman. Surely she'd been pursued by eligible men, had been offered plenty of opportunities to get involved in a serious relationship. And she had to be pulling in a decent salary, working for Mattson.

Yet she chose to live a spartan, barebones life.

Alone.

As he turned onto the highway and accelerated toward church, the same question echoed in his mind again.

Why?

But given her reticence, he had a feeling it might be a long time—if ever—before he had an answer.

Kristen pulled into the parking lot next to the visitor center at Prairie Creek Redwoods State Park, slid out of her car and drew a calming breath of the spruce-scented air. The short drive from Starfish Bay had been a pleasant start to her Friday afternoon—and a nice break from her first hectic week at the inn. Between training the assistant concierges, preparing for the grand opening in three weeks and coordinating the open house Louis Mattson had decided to throw for Starfish Bay residents, she'd been working fourteen-hour days.

Technically, she was working now, too. How could she recommend area attractions to guests without first checking them out herself? Though given the gorgeous setting and the comfortable jeans she'd donned, she felt as if she was playing hooky.

Pressing the auto lock on her key chain, she followed the sidewalk to the low-slung, wood-shingled visitor center tucked among the giant redwoods, ticking off her agenda in her mind. She'd scope out the place, gather up some brochures and trail maps and get the lowdown on park highlights from someone knowledgeable about Prairie Creek. Then she'd tool down the ten-mile-long Newton B. Drury Scenic Parkway for an up-close view of the towering trees.

Poking her head into the right wing of the structure, she gave the small, deserted museum a quick scan and retreated. On the other side of the building, she found a small gift shop and bookstore as well as an unstaffed information desk.

Taking the Ranger on Duty sign at face value, she wandered over to peruse the trail map displayed on a bulletin board, leaning close for a better look as she waited for a staff member to show up.

Three minutes later, a familiar resonant

baritone voice with the hint of a Southern accent spoke behind her. "Can I help you?"

She swung around. Sure enough, it was her landlord. At least she thought it was her landlord. But the gray shirt, dark green slacks and distinctive flat-brimmed beige hat threw her.

Clint Nolan was a park ranger?

Her gaze flicked to the nametag on the left pocket flap of his shirt.

Yeah, he was.

Given his muscles and toned physique, she'd guessed his occupation involved physical labor. But a ranger hadn't been on the list of professions she'd considered. Genevieve or Lindsey at the Mercantile could have cleared up the mystery, of course, if she'd been able to think of a casual way to introduce the topic—and if she hadn't been afraid such a query would suggest she had a personal interest in the man.

Which of course she didn't.

Now she had her answer, anyway.

"This is a surprise." Clint stayed where

he was, hovering on the threshold, his expression guarded...and curious.

"Yeah. For me, too." She tucked her fingers in the front pockets of her jeans and gave him a once-over. How come his shoulders seemed broader in his uniform shirt? And he looked taller, too. Was he wearing boots?

As she started to check out that theory, he spoke again.

"Is there something I can help you with?"

She jerked her chin back up, and her cheeks warmed. He'd asked her that once already, hadn't he?

"Yes. I'm, uh, checking out the area attractions so I know what to recommend to our guests. This park is an obvious choice, but I wanted to talk to someone about which trails to suggest, flora and fauna to watch for, safety concerns. That kind of thing."

He eased past her in the cramped space to circle around behind the information desk, leaving a subtle woodsy, masculine scene in his wake.

Her pulse spiked.

Rats.

The last thing she needed was an appealing landlord. The proximity of their living quarters could cause problems—like tempting her to violate her no-strings rule.

She needed to quash this. Fast.

As Clint pulled out a trail map and opened it on the counter between them, she did her best to focus on his comments about Fern Canyon, Gold Bluffs Beach, Roosevelt elk, whale watching and the Rhododendron Trail. But he didn't grab her full attention until he mentioned mountain lions.

"There are mountain lions in the park?" She stared at him.

"Yes. Along with plenty of other wildlife. This is their home."

"Does that mean hiking is dangerous?"

"Not usually. But once in a great while, if a lion is sick or hungry, it will attack humans. It happened here a few years before I became a ranger. If your guests are worried, we do offer interpretive talks and guided walks in season. And here are a few brochures with tips for wildlife encounters." He pulled a handful from beneath the desk and passed them over. "I wouldn't discourage people from exploring on their own, though. Hiking in the redwoods is an amazing experience."

"Okay." She'd have to think about this one. On Maui, the only danger she'd had to warn guests about was jellyfish. "So can you recommend some popular trails in the easy, moderate and difficult range?" She tucked the brochures in her shoulder tote.

"Sure. Brown Creek is a moderate trail." He indicated it on the map. "If you really want to get a feel for what that means, though, it would be helpful to do some hiking yourself." He shot her an appraising look, and she read the challenge in his eyes.

It did not sit well.

"I was about to go check out reports of a downed tree on that trail. You're welcome to come along. Your sport shoes will handle the terrain with no problem." He folded up the map, watching her.

She eyed him. First the rustic remark about his apartment. Now this…dare. Did he think she was a pansy because of her high-end resort job?

No matter the basis for his opinion, it might be fun to throw him for a loop.

With a smile, she picked up the gauntlet. "Okay."

The slightly arched brow above his left eye was the only visible sign she'd succeeded in her attempt to confound him.

"It's an easy path to follow, so if you get tired you can always turn back without fear of getting lost." He handed her a trail map.

"Good to know. But I've got a fair amount of stamina." She tucked the map in the pocket of her jeans. "Shall I meet you at the trailhead?"

"We can take a park vehicle. Give me two minutes to round up someone to watch the desk."

"No problem. I'll wait for you in the parking lot."

As she turned away, Clint pulled out his cell. That was when Kristen noticed the gun on his belt. First an ax, now a side-arm. Maybe the man had an oversupply of testosterone.

Then again, in a forest where mountain lions roamed, he might not be a bad guy to have around.

Besides, she was looking forward to showing him she didn't neatly fit into whatever stereotype he'd assigned to her.

As for why she cared what he thought—she'd leave that question for another day.

Chapter Four

Clint grabbed his jacket from a hook in the staff area of the visitor center and shoved his arms into the sleeves. Kristen Andrews was full of surprises. Take those sport shoes. She didn't seem the type to appear in public in such plebeian footwear. And jeans didn't fit his image of her, either. Oh, sure, designer jeans, maybe. The kind women like her wore with fancy boots or high heels. But he wouldn't have expected her to go for the off-the-rack, rough-and-ready style she was modeling today. Those were the kind people who wanted to do more than look pretty wore.

Still, she did look pretty.

And a little less like Lisa in that rugged attire. Which was a plus.

Wasn't it?

Unsure of that answer, he exited the ranger station and followed the path toward the parking lot. Pre-season, there were plenty of open spaces. He spotted Kristen immediately, behind what appeared to be a spanking-new silver Accord. Another surprise. She drove a workhorse car, not a fancy BMW like…

He cut off that thought—cold.

Once he had a clear view of her, however, he stopped abruptly and stared.

She had one foot propped on the bumper while she laced up a hiking boot that was definitely not spanking new.

Huh.

Lisa's idea of a hike had been a trek through the mall to Neiman Marcus.

Given her well-broken-in boots, no wonder Kristen had agreed to accompany him.

She looked up as he approached, and he had no trouble interpreting her smug "gotcha" smile. "I'm about set." She pulled the bow taut, then reached into the trunk and retrieved a daypack.

As she pulled it out, he realized he'd left his own backpack in the ranger station.

That was a first.

But he wasn't about to retrace his steps to retrieve it. That would only confirm she'd discombobulated him.

"You're very prepared." He fished his keys out of his pocket.

"I try to be." She closed her trunk and gave him a steady look. "For all contingencies. I wasn't sure I'd hike today, but since you've offered to be my guide, why not? Where's your car?"

He gestured toward an SUV bearing the logo of the California Department of Parks and Recreation. She flicked a look at the USNPS leather band on his hat.

"Do you work for the National Park Service or for California?"

Impressive. Few people caught that distinction.

"The National Park Service. There are several state parks within Redwood National Park, and they're managed cooperatively by the two organizations. Ready?" He gestured toward the SUV.

She slung her daypack over one shoulder and took off toward the vehicle. He followed, intending to open the door for her. But she'd circled the vehicle and was already climbing in as he rounded the hood.

He got the message.

Kristen Andrews was an independent woman. She didn't need his help.

Fine. No problem.

Correcting his course, he circled back to the driver side, pulled open the door and took his place behind the wheel.

"How far is this trail?" She snapped her seat belt closed.

"A couple of miles. Have you ever been to the redwoods?"

"No."

"Then get set. You're in for a treat. The scenic parkway is well named."

She settled back without comment.

But a few minutes later, as the narrow

road began to wind through the soaring giants, she leaned forward in her seat.

"Oh, my." The words came out in a hushed, almost reverent whisper as she eyeballed the girth of the massive trunks, then craned her neck, trying to see the tops. "This is amazing! I love how the sunlight slants through the branches. And everything is so green and lush! It feels… primeval."

So she appreciated the wonders of nature. Another point in her favor—not that he was keeping score.

"This is an old-growth area. There are close to three hundred groves like this in the park. The parkway is a great introduction to the redwoods, but nothing beats walking among them, as you'll soon discover."

Quiet fell in the SUV as she continued to gape at the trees.

Once at the Brown Creek trailhead, he pulled off the road and parked. Before he could offer to get her door, she was out of the car, head tipped back, scanning the distant treetops.

He slid out, locked the vehicle and joined her as she shrugged into her daypack. "Would you like me to carry that?"

She adjusted it and settled the straps on her shoulders. "No, thanks. I'm used to it."

How come he wasn't surprised?

"I take it you've done some hiking."

"A fair amount. A lot of our guests enjoy exploring the natural beauty around the Mattson resorts, and I can offer better rec-ommendations if I experience the sights personally."

"Was there much hiking on Maui?" He gestured toward the trail, and she preceded him down the needle-carpeted path, set-ting an impressive pace.

"More than you might think. Hiking the summit of Haleakala Crater is awesome. And farther afield, the Na Pali Coast on Kauai and Molokai's Kalaupapa trail are fabulous."

Okay. The lady had totally suckered him. Two of those trails were in national parks, and he'd read enough about all three to know they were very strenuous—the equivalent of a black ski run, minimum.

"Do all concierges take their jobs so seriously?"

Her throaty chuckle floated back to him. "No. But this isn't work to me. I like the outdoors. I always have. Lucky thing, since I spent most of my youth helping my parents run their small lakeside resort in Wisconsin." She pulled up short and pointed to the ground on the side of the trail. "What's that?"

Still digesting the new information she'd offered, he closed the distance between them and checked out the six-inch-long, neon-yellow creature.

"A banana slug. They're common here."

"Boy, he's a bright little guy." She dropped to one knee and bent down to get up close and personal with the slug. "Hmm. He has antennas." She ran a finger gently down the length of the body. "And he's slippery."

The elegant concierge from Inn at The Point had touched a slug.

One by one, Clint's preconceived notions about her were crumbling. No way on earth would Lisa have gotten close to a slimy creature like this, let alone touched one.

Kristen stood again and started forward, following the narrow, descending path through a profusion of giant ferns.

"Wow. This is just like *Jurassic Park*. I wouldn't be surprised if we ran into a dinosaur."

Now it was his turn to chuckle. "No chance of that, although part of the movie was filmed here. But how about a marbled murrelet? It's not as rare as a dinosaur, but it is a threatened species. This is your lucky day. I don't often spot them."

Stopping, she glanced around and lowered her voice. "That's a bird, right? Where is it?"

He moved beside her and bent close, pointing to the small, black-beaked bird with a black crown and back. "In the tree at two o'clock. Twelve feet up."

She lifted her head, following the direction of his finger. Her soft hair brushed his chin, and the distinctive fragrance he'd noticed the day she'd checked out his apartment enveloped him. Then, he'd termed it exotic. Now it struck him more as interesting—and appealing.

His pulse did an odd hesitation step.

"Oh, I see it!"

As she spoke, the bird took wing and disappeared—giving him an excellent excuse to step back…and regroup.

She eyed him. "You know a lot about this area, but you're not a native, are you?"

"No. I spent most of my life in South Carolina."

"Aha! I knew I detected a slight Southern accent." She turned and resumed walking. "So what brought you out here?"

He followed more slowly, choosing his words with care. He hadn't shared his real reason for relocating with anyone in Starfish Bay, and he didn't intend to start now.

"I wanted a change of pace, and I've always loved the outdoors. We took a family vacation out here when I was a kid, and I fell in love with the redwoods. I always said I'd come back. Three years ago I made good on that vow."

It was his standard answer. One everyone he'd recited it to had accepted at face value.

Until now.

"That's a dramatic change, moving all the way across the country. What about the life you left behind?"

He gave himself a few seconds to formulate a noncommittal answer. "It was time to make a change."

She didn't respond at once. If he was lucky, she'd take the hint and let the subject of his past drop.

"So did you work for the National Park Service back there, too?"

Obviously this wasn't his lucky day.

"No." He clenched his fists. Flexed his fingers. Kept breathing. "I was a police officer."

She shot a look over her shoulder at his gun. "Is that what you do here, as a ranger? Enforce the law?"

"For the most part I do interpretation and education. Law enforcement is secondary."

"How come?"

This was getting stickier by the minute.

"I used my criminal justice degree for ten years. I figured I better switch gears before my forestry and marine biology degrees got dusty."

She stopped and swiveled toward him. "You have three degrees?"

At her incredulous question, he stopped, too, keeping a safe distance between them. Why had he told her that? He hadn't mentioned his academic credentials to any of the Starfish Bay residents he'd known for three years, and he'd just met this woman a few weeks ago.

But that was a puzzle he'd have to tackle later. Right now, he needed to employ some diversionary tactics.

"I double majored in criminal justice and forestry in college. I worked on the marine biology degree in my spare time. Like I said, I've always enjoyed the outdoors."

"I'm impressed."

He shrugged. "Don't be. It's no effort to do something you love." He gestured down the trail. "Let's keep moving. I need to check out that tree."

For the next twenty-five minutes, Kristen kept up a steady pace—up, down, ducking under and around trees…it didn't matter. Her speed never varied. She only slowed when he called her attention to various points of interest, including the rhododendrons that were about to burst into bloom. His new tenant was in great condition.

Must be the yoga.

When they at last arrived at the downed tree, Kristen spotted it first as she rounded a curve. It was hard to miss, considering it was blocking the trail.

"Oh my word. It's a giant." She slowed as she approached the massive trunk. "That is so sad. What on earth made it fall over?" She ran her fingers reverently over the furrowed bark.

"A combination of wet soil and strong winds, probably. It may have been leaning, too, which would have left it more susceptible to uprooting." He gestured toward the huge exposed root structure in the distance, down the long expanse of trunk. "Redwoods don't have large, anchoring taproots. To compensate, they send out surface roots that interlock with the roots of their neighbors. That connection to other trees gives them stability. But it didn't save this one."

"How old do you think it was?"

"Seven hundred years, give or take a few decades." He inspected the blocked trail. "We'll have to send out a crew to cut a pass-through here tomorrow. This is one of the most popular trails, and the summer vacation crowd is about to descend. Are you ready to start back?"

She hesitated, her hand still on the tree. "I feel like we should have a moment of silence or something. The end of a seven-hundred-year life is significant." She gestured toward a plank bench they'd passed a few dozen feet back up the path, tucked in among the giant ferns. "Could we sit there for a few minutes? I brought some water and snacks."

A wake for a tree. That was a new concept.

But it was nice to know the lady had a soft heart.

"Sure. Give me a minute to call the office with the particulars." He pulled his radio off his belt.

"I'll wait on the bench." After giving the tree a final pat, she retraced their route.

As Clint punched in the numbers and watched her go, he found himself wondering what other surprises his new tenant might have in store for him.

And was forced to admit he was looking forward to finding out.

Kristen let her daypack slip off her shoulders, set it beside the weathered bench and sat. Back by the downed tree, Clint was angled away from her, still talking on the radio.

Thank goodness the man had no idea she was keeping him here under false pretenses.

Yes, she did feel bad about the death of the majestic tree. But she'd seen a lot of downed trees during their hike, and Clint had explained that they had amazing powers of regeneration, sending up vertical sprouts from roots growing near the surface. This tree probably had many such offspring.

No, her suggestion to pause for a few minutes was motivated more by curiosity about him. While the hike had been instructive, giving her new information about his background, it had also raised more questions.

He'd been a cop, then changed careers midstream and moved across the country. He'd claimed it was because he loved the outdoors, because he'd visited this place as a kid and always said he'd come back. Yet people didn't leave everything behind without a superstrong motivation.

There was a piece of his story he hadn't shared. Why?

Also, as far as she could see, he was unattached. He wore no ring, nor did he appear to have a steady girlfriend. He hadn't entertained any visitors at his house since she'd moved in. He seemed to lead a very solitary life. Why?

As for the handful of personal questions she'd asked today, he'd answered them but offered no additional information. Talking about private stuff seemed to be off-limits. Why?

Perhaps if she got him chatting in a casual, relaxed atmosphere he'd answer a few of the whys running through her mind.

Keeping an eye on the mystery man, she lifted the daypack onto her lap, unzipped the main compartment and pulled out two bottles of water. After setting them on the bench, she opened the side compartment and took out a bag of trail mix and two granola bars. She arranged the provisions in the middle of the bench and returned the pack to the ground beside her.

In the distance, Clint slipped the radio onto his belt and walked toward her.

"You did come prepared." He surveyed the mini buffet as he took a seat on the opposite side of the bench. "What else is in there?" He gestured to the daypack.

"First-aid kit, compass, flashlight, matches, cell phone, digital camera, a small pair of binoculars and rain gear."

"The cell phone won't do you much good here. Spotty reception. But you're far better prepared than most of the hikers I meet." He picked up one of the bottles of water and lifted it in salute as he unscrewed the cap.

"You learn—sometimes the hard way."

"Can I assume there's a story there?" He took a swig of water.

"You can. I got dehydrated once on a desert hike. It wasn't pretty." She chose one of the granola bars and ripped open the wrapping.

"Where was that?"

"New Mexico, while I was working for one of the Mattson resorts near Santa Fe."

"You've been around."

She bit into the granola bar and lifted one shoulder as she chewed. "I go where they send me."

"What happened to the resort in Wisconsin? No interest in the family business?"

She continued to chew, but the sweet cinnamon flavor soured on her tongue. This conversation was supposed to be about him, not her.

On the other hand, maybe if she shared a little more about her background, he'd open up, too.

"I would have gone back, but my parents had to sell it when I was twenty to raise funds for my dad's cancer treatments—which weren't successful. He died a year later. My mom still lives in the closest town, near my brother. I go back when I can, but it's not the same." Even after all these years, it hurt to talk about that painful period in her life. Loss of her childhood home. Loss of the dream of running the family business. Loss of her father. Loss of...

Ruthlessly she stifled that last thought.

She needed to get this conversation back on track. *Her* track.

Forcing herself to refocus, she turned toward Clint—and found him looking at her hand. The one that was squeezing the life out of the granola bar.

The man didn't miss a thing.

She loosened her grip, peeled back some more of the paper and took another bite she didn't want. "So what about you? Do you have family back in South Carolina? And where did you live there?"

He didn't rush to answer. Instead, he draped an arm along the back of the bench and took another swig of water. The forest was silent around them for so long she wondered if he was going to respond—but at last he did.

"Charleston. My sister and her family still live there, as does my dad. My mom passed away ten years ago."

"Do you get back often?"

"No."

Why not?

Kristen didn't voice that question, but he must have read it in her eyes, because he spoke again.

"They get out here now and then."

So he wasn't estranged from his family. For some reason, she found that reassuring.

She fingered a frond of the giant fern beside the bench. "My brother's not married yet, but I'm looking forward to having nieces and nephews. Sounds like you have a few."

"Two. A boy and girl." He studied her for a moment. "So you like children?"

He'd done it again. Turned the focus back to her—and to a topic she didn't want to discuss.

"Sure. Who doesn't like kids?" She crumpled the remainder of her granola bar and the wrapper in her fist, finished off her own water in several long gulps and bent to stow everything in the daypack, hiding her face from his view. "Are you ready to go?"

"Yeah." He handed her his empty water bottle.

She stuffed it in the main compartment, zipped the pack shut and rose, keeping her back to him as she gave the downed tree one final sweep. "You know, impressive as the redwoods are upright, you get a whole different perspective on them when they're down. And maybe even a greater appreciation for their nobility."

Behind her, she heard him stand. "That can be true of more than trees."

At his quiet comment, she turned to him, her fingers clenched around the straps of her pack. He had the most intense, delving eyes. The kind that could strip away layers of pretense and see into a person's soul, where heartbreak dwelled.

Or perhaps she was being too fanciful.

Because if he could see into her soul, he wouldn't find nobility. He'd find cowardice and selfishness and secrets even God couldn't forgive.

And he'd want nothing to do with her.

Throat tightening, she hefted the pack

into a snugger position, brushed past him and took off down the trail.

They didn't talk on the hike back, and the return drive to the visitor center was mostly silent as well. He, too, seemed reluctant to share any more personal history.

When he pulled up beside her car, she opened the door and slid out the instant the SUV came to a stop. "Thanks for the guided hike."

"No problem." He rested his forearm on the wheel. "I didn't get a chance back there to tell you I was sorry about the loss of your family resort, but I am. It's hard to give up a future you've planned."

Somehow she sensed he had personal insight into that experience. That his future, too, had been different than the one he'd anticipated. But in what way?

Before she could think of a reply, he put the SUV in gear. "Drive safe going back."

"Yeah. I will. See you around." She shut the door and stepped back.

An instant later, he pulled away.

Slowly Kristen walked to her car, deposited the daypack in her trunk and changed back into her sport shoes. By the time she slid behind the wheel, he'd disappeared down the road.

Two minutes later, as she exited past the herd of Roosevelt elk that had come to graze in the pasture near the visitor center, she couldn't help wondering what Clint's real story was. Why had an intelligent, educated, good-looking man left his life behind and moved to tiny Starfish Bay? Why did he never go home? Was there an unhappy romance in his past, perhaps? Possibly a divorce? Some other secret buried deep in his heart?

Frowning, Kristen merged onto 101. Given his reticence, it wasn't likely the man himself would provide the answers to any of those questions.

But she had other sources. Genevieve seemed to know everything about everybody in Starfish Bay. And Lindsey was privy to a lot, too, since the Mercantile's coffee nook was a social hub in the tiny town. It might be possible to ferret out a few details with some discreet questions.

As for why she cared about her landlord's background—she'd leave that troubling question for another day, too.

Chapter Five

"An open house! How lovely! Lillian, come look at this!" Genevieve called the last sentence to her sister through the pass-through in the café that separated the stool-lined counter from the kitchen, then turned back to Kristen. "That Louis Mattson is so thoughtful. He never fails to stop in here for a bite and a visit when he's in town. And inviting all the residents to a preview of the inn before it opens—everyone will be thrilled! We've all been dying for a peek inside."

"What is it, Genevieve? I have pies to bake, and Barbara will be stopping by any minute to whip up a couple of her carrot cakes for us." Lillian bustled through the swinging door off to one side, wiping her flour-dusted hands on a towel. "Hello, Kristen."

"Hi, Lillian." She smiled at the two energetic seventy-something sisters, who bore absolutely no resemblance to one another. While Genevieve was short and a bit rounded, with white hair she always wore in a soft chignon, Lillian was tall and spare, and her cropped dark hair sported only a few streaks of gray.

"Look at this." Genevieve handed Lillian the flyer Kristen had just delivered. "Won't that be fun? I haven't been to a cocktail party in years. I'll have to dig out that fancy dress I wore to the wedding we attended last time we went home to Georgia."

Lillian scanned the flyer. "Goodness. It's been quite a while since Starfish Bay had such a fancy party."

"Like never," Genevieve declared.

"In any case, I expect everyone will have

a fine time. It's a very thoughtful gesture." Lillian smiled at Kristen.

"I was hoping you'd post this in the café. Everyone in town seems to stop in here once or twice a week. I also put one on the bulletin board at the Mercantile, and a few other businesses are displaying them in their windows, too."

"We'd be happy to." Genevieve took the flyer from her sister. "We'll tape it by the cash register, where all our customers will see it. And we'll talk it up, too."

"Well, back to work for me. Nice to see you, Kristen." Lifting a hand in farewell, Lillian hurried back toward the kitchen.

"Speaking of working…you must have pulled weekend duty if you're delivering these." Genevieve waved the flyer. "Though I suppose concierges work a lot of Saturdays."

"I'm not on the clock today. I just wanted to get these out as soon as possible."

And ask a few of the questions about my landlord that popped up during our hike yesterday.

So far, however, she'd been batting zero with those questions. Lindsey genuinely hadn't seemed to know as much as Kristen did about Clint, and after the owner of the Mercantile had commented that the man kept to himself and everyone respected his privacy, Kristen had let the topic drop. She hadn't wanted the other woman to think she was nosy.

Even if she was.

If anyone in Starfish Bay had any additional background information on Clint, however, it would be Genevieve. Might as well give it one more try.

"So do you think everyone will come?" She spooned a few M&M's out of the always-overflowing bowl beside the cash register, dumped them in her palm and popped one in her mouth.

"Are you kidding? The inn's been the talk of the town for months. The whole place will be there with bells on."

"I suppose we'll miss a few residents, though, if they work odd hours. Lindsey says they'll close the Mercantile early that night, but I'm not sure about people like Clint. I guess rangers keep unusual hours."

"Not this time of year. He's mostly nine to five, though I know he works some weekends and then gets a day off during the week. But that will change in high season, starting next month. Still, he might not come. He's on the quiet side, and he keeps to himself."

"I noticed that. I live above him, and our paths don't cross very often. Plus, I rarely hear any noise from below. He seems nice enough, though." Kristen strove for a casual, conversational tone.

"Salt of the earth. He was a great help during the Save the Point campaign, quietly doing what needed to be done, never taking any credit. And he's put in a lot of personal hours on the interpretive trail, too. Nice man. Too bad he's all alone."

The perfect opening.

"Is he?" Kristen adopted an indifferent air, feigning an interest in the chalkboard behind the counter that listed the day's special. "I thought he might have a girl-friend."

"Not that I know of." Genevieve leaned close and dropped her voice to a conspiratorial whisper. "If you ask me, there's a tragic romance in that man's past."

At the candid comment, which mirrored her speculation from yesterday, Kristen gave up any pretense of reading the daily special. "Why would you think that?"

"He has the look."

"What look?"

"The one that's sad, real deep in his eyes. Like he's lost something—or someone—important to him. I've seen it before." The older woman sized her up with a shrewd expression.

Kristen's palms started to sweat.

Did the café owner have psychic powers?

She juggled the M&M's in her hand—hoping they lived up to their claim of melting in the mouth, not the hand—as she debated her options. She could make a fast exit…but she might not have the opportunity again to pick Genevieve's brain without raising suspicion.

Better to see if she could refocus the conversation on Clint and glean a tad more information before she escaped.

"It *is* interesting that he moved so far from home."

"And left everything—and everyone—behind." Genevieve gave a knowing nod, as if that proved her point. "From what little he's said about his past, I gather he was close to his family. There's a woman at the root of his cross-country trek, mark my words."

"Maybe he's a widower or went through a nasty divorce."

"Nope. He's never been married." Genevieve rummaged through a drawer behind the counter and pulled out a tape dispenser.

For once the garrulous café proprietor didn't elaborate, forcing Kristen to press for details. "How do you know?"

Genevieve tore off two pieces of tape and

attached them to the flyer, then affixed the whole thing to the front of the counter. "He came in on my anniversary a few months ago, when I was feeling kind of low. I still miss my Sam something fierce, even after fifteen years, and it's always worse on our anniversary. Anyway, we got to talking, and he told me that while he's never walked down the aisle, he hopes to meet the right woman someday. So there you have it." She pressed the tape in place and stepped back to examine her handiwork.

Mulling over that news, Kristen hoisted her purse higher and prepared to leave. "Thanks for posting that, Genevieve."

"Happy to do it." The woman propped her hands on her ample hips and studied Kristen. "So how are you settling in here in our tiny town? Starfish Bay must be a lot different than Maui."

"Yes, but it has its charms."

"Must have been hard to leave such a

tropical paradise, though. Not to mention all your friends."

"Not really. I'm a Wisconsin girl. The tropical climate always felt a bit artificial to me. And I was only there three years, so I didn't make many friends. With the long hours I work, there isn't much opportunity to socialize."

Nor did she want to. It was easier to leave when the time came if you didn't connect with people or put down roots.

"No boyfriend, then?"

"No."

"Well…" The woman beamed at her, obviously pleased by that news for some reason. "I'm sure you'll have the chance to mingle with some nice, eligible young men at the inn—or closer to home." Genevieve winked at her.

Oh, great.

The owner of the Orchid Café was now playing matchmaker.

She was out of here.

"Considering the demands of my job, I

doubt I'll have the time or energy to do much dating for the foreseeable future." She edged toward the door.

"Sam and I didn't date at first, either. We just kept running into each other around town when out of the blue, sparks started to fly. And there wasn't a thing we could do about it. That's how romance happens sometimes. Bang. Hits you between the eyes, when you least expect it."

Apparently fairy tales were on the menu at the Orchid, along with the sisters' famous pot roast.

But Kristen didn't have an appetite for either at the moment.

"See you later, Genevieve." She pushed through the door without waiting for a reply.

Yet as she walked toward her car, she had to admit the older woman was right about one thing. Sparks did have a tendency to fly when you least expected them, and there wasn't a whole lot you could do about that except ignore them—or avoid the source.

Which was exactly how she intended to deal with her landlord. She'd do her best to see that their paths intersected as seldom as possible, and when she couldn't avoid him, she'd make a concerted effort to disregard the annoying sparks that were beginning to fly.

Because sparks could lead to romance, as Genevieve had noted.

And romance wasn't on her agenda for Starfish Bay.

From his spot beside the shimmering infinity pool, sheltered on three sides by the low-slung Inn at The Point, Clint gazed around at the Starfish Bay residents enjoying the food, drink and ambience as a jazz ensemble played softly in the background.

He hadn't been any more thrilled than Lindsey at the Mercantile once they'd gotten wind of Mattson's plans to develop The Point, but he had to admit the man had kept his promise. The inn blended with the natural surroundings, and the developer had even restored and rebuilt—on a smaller scale—the town's beloved Starfish Bay Chapel, once the only structure on The Point.

Mattson was also on hand today, circulating among the guests, making everyone feel welcome. No question about it; the man was a class act.

"So what do you think?"

At the question, Clint turned to find Scott Walsh, the project foreman, standing behind him with his new wife and stepson. Clint smiled at Cindy and Jarrod, who'd lived in Starfish Bay far longer than he had. It was nice to see the young widow looking so happy—and nice to know happy endings were possible.

For some people.

"Spectacular." Clint kept his smile in place, but it was an effort. "Hi, Cindy. Jarrod."

"Man, that pool is awesome." The thirteen-year-old continued to ogle both the setting and the pool.

Scott grinned. "But it was a bear to excavate and build."

"I'll bet." Clint's lips quirked up at the man's comment. Scott seemed like a decent guy. He'd stopped by several times while Clint was working on the interpretive trail to check on the progress and offer assistance.

Lindsey strolled over, her husband, Nate, in tow. The man snagged a stuffed mushroom cap from the tray of a waiter who was passing out hors d'oeuvres.

"I have to admit this turned out a lot better than I expected when we organized the Save the Point campaign." Lindsey surveyed the pool and the elegant stone, glass and wood structure. "It's very tasteful and low-key. Plus, we kept the chapel." She glanced at the white steeple, peeking above the roof of the inn as it soared to the sky from its own private garden on the other side of the structure.

"And the bench," Nate added, giving her shoulder a squeeze.

She nestled closer to her husband, and the look that passed between them tightened Clint's throat. That was true love—as was the squeeze Scott gave his wife's fingers.

He felt like a third wheel.

"I think I'll wander over to the other side and see if I can scrounge up some heartier food." He tried for a lighthearted tone despite his sudden melancholy. "Will you excuse me?"

"Sure. Make the most of it. You won't see a party like this in Starfish Bay again anytime soon." Lindsey flashed him a grin.

As he circled the pool, Clint helped himself to a stuffed mushroom, a mini quiche and a scallop wrapped in bacon secured with a toothpick, motivated more by the persuasive smiles of the proffering waiters than by hunger.

Halfway around, Louis Mattson flagged him down and shook his hand. "I'm glad you could make it, Clint. So what do you think of the place?"

"It's amazing—and out of my league. But it's nice to see how the other half lives for a couple of hours." He took a marinated shrimp from the tray a waiter offered. "The food is spectacular, by the way."

"Glad to hear it."

"The music's nice, too. You throw a great party."

"I can't take any credit for the arrangements. I left those in the capable hands of the inn's event planner and head concierge. Ah…here she is now." The man leaned sideways and flagged her down over Clint's shoulder.

Wiping his hands on the cocktail napkin, Clint turned. In the two weeks since their impromptu hike, he'd seen nothing of his tenant. Nor had he heard much. A car door closing when she left for work in the morning—early. Another door closing when she arrived home at night—late. Aside from that, the muffled sound of water running and a few squeaks from the floorboards were the only audible signs of her presence. The woman put in incredible hours.

And the hectic pace of her life showed. Though she'd applied her makeup with a liberal hand, she hadn't been able to totally mask the shadows under her lower lashes.

She gave him a smile that was more PR than genuine and turned her attention to Mattson. "I hope you're enjoying the party."

"It's wonderful. And more importantly, our guests agree. I've heard nothing but rave reviews about the food, the band, the ambience. Clint was just adding his compliments." The man leaned sideways and waved at some new arrivals. "The sisters from the Orchid are here. I want to go over and say hello." He reached out to shake Clint's hand again. "Eat some more of that food. You, too." He smiled at Kristen. "Might as well enjoy the party you planned."

He walked away, leaving silence in his

wake. While he wasn't the most gregarious person, Clint could usually make small talk if pressed. But for whatever reason, he couldn't think of a thing to say.

Desperate to fill the awkward lull, he stopped a passing waiter and helped himself to two mini quiches, passing one to Kristen.

She tried to demur. "I don't usually eat at these kinds of events. There are always too many details to see to."

"Everything seems to be under control. Like the man said, you might as well enjoy the party you planned."

Acquiescing, she took the quiche and nibbled at it.

"Would you like a drink?"

"No. That's definitely verboten when I'm on duty."

"How about a soda?"

"Thanks. I'm fine." She took another dainty bite of the quiche he'd demolished in one gulp. "This is very tasty. But then, the food at Mattson properties is always stellar."

"And fancy."

"That, too." She finished off the quiche and wiped her hands on the cocktail napkin he supplied. "But our guests like to explore other dining options, too. I have no problem sending them to the Orchid for some home cooking and local flavor, but I wish there was somewhere else close by."

"What about Jaz's?"

Three beats of silence passed as she regarded him, her expression wary. "The biker bar at the edge of town? In the old gas station?"

"Yeah."

Her squint, and the tilt of her head, conveyed her skepticism. "I don't think our clientele would go for that."

"The food's great."

"Even so…"

"Have you ever been inside?"

"No."

"You might not want to judge by appearances." When she didn't respond, he spoke again. "If you want to test it out, I'd be happy to meet you there for lunch tomorrow. But I'm afraid you won't find anything fancy like sushi."

That got the same reaction as had his rustic reference during her apartment-hunting visit. Her chin lifted and he could feel her bristling. Now why had he baited her again? You'd think he'd have learned his lesson.

"As a matter of fact, I've never been a fan of sushi—or roadkill."

His lips twitched. Witty comeback.

"Jaz doesn't serve roadkill—at least, not that I know of. But I can vouch for his burgers. They're the best I've ever had. He also throws a mean pizza. You won't find quiche on the menu, however. So it's not exactly Inn at The Point fare."

She pursed her lips and considered him. Part of him hoped she'd decline. The other part hoped she'd accept.

He wasn't certain which part he wanted to win.

All he knew was that since their hike two weeks ago, he'd found himself thinking about her far too often—and hoping he'd have another excuse to spend time with her, even if she did remind him of Lisa.

The resemblance was especially remarkable today. Kristen's sleek, classy black cocktail dress, its modest cowl neckline offsetting the low dip in the back, was the very kind of outfit Lisa might have worn.

"Okay. You're on. What time shall I meet you?"

His pulse edged up. The stunning woman across from him, who seemed as comfortable in a designer cocktail dress as she did in jeans and hiking boots, was willing to join him for lunch. His mood took a decided upswing—answering the question about whether he'd wanted her to accept or not.

"Will one o'clock work? That will give

me a chance to get home from church and change."

Her lips curved into a smile. "One's fine. I take it the attire at Jaz's is casual."

"Very. Why don't we go together? That is, if you don't mind riding in a truck."

"I've ridden in plenty of trucks." A waiter signaled to her, and she wadded the napkin in her fingers. "Duty calls. See you tomorrow."

He watched her walk away, the filmy fabric of her dress rippling in the breeze.

A waiter approached with a tray of champagne, and on impulse Clint picked up a flute. He didn't usually indulge, but for whatever reason, he felt in a celebratory mood.

Raising the glass in silent salute to his tenant, he sipped the bubbly liquid and launched a mental countdown until lunch tomorrow, hoping anticipation wouldn't keep him tossing all night.

He'd felt the same with Lisa at the beginning, too, though. She'd been classy and upscale as well. He'd never been able to figure out what she'd seen in him, never understood why she'd fallen in love with him. So when things ended, he hadn't been surprised—though her motive for dumping him had had nothing to do with differences in class.

It had been all about hate.

His stomach clenched, and he took another swig of champagne. He'd never blamed her for walking out. Never blamed her for her inability to forgive him. How could he, when he'd never been able to forgive himself?

But just because Kristen reminded him of Lisa didn't mean things with her had to come to the same dismal end.

At least he hoped not.

Chapter Six

At one o'clock sharp on Sunday, Kristen stepped onto the landing outside her apartment, locked the door and descended the stairs.

She found Clint waiting for her beside his truck, one hip propped against the door, arms crossed.

"Am I late?" She knew she wasn't. Could it be he was just anxious to see her?

When her heart skipped a beat at that possibility, she frowned in annoyance.

Get over it, Kristen. No strings, remember? This is a work-related research outing, nothing more.

"No. You're very punctual." He pushed

off from the truck and gave her a quick once-over.

She reciprocated. Her jeans weren't as faded as his, and her soft cashmere sweater was definitely nicer than his black cotton shirt with sleeves rolled to the elbows.

At least he wasn't wearing a scuffed leather jacket or torn jeans.

"Is this too dressy for Jaz's?" She gestured to her attire.

"It'll do." He opened the passenger door and ushered her in.

She climbed aboard. He closed the door behind her, circled the hood and took his own seat.

"I'd have been happy to drive." She pulled the seat belt across her lap.

He inserted the key. "I don't mind."

"You don't trust me behind the wheel, do you?" She snapped the belt in place as he put the truck in gear and started down the drive.

"I didn't say that."

"You didn't deny it, either."

One side of his mouth twitched, as if he was trying to suppress a smile. "True."

"I'm actually a very good driver. I've never gotten a ticket or had an accident."

"The ticket I can understand."

She sent him a wary look. "What's that supposed to mean?"

"Look in the mirror."

She narrowed her eyes as his insinuation registered. "Are you suggesting I might have used my feminine wiles to get out of a ticket?"

"Let me ask you this. You said you've never gotten a ticket. But have you ever been stopped by a cop?"

"Yes."

"I rest my case."

She blew out an exasperated breath and glared at him. "For the record, I never batted my eyelashes at any of those cops."

"Ah. Multiple stops." His lips flexed again.

Kristen's irritation swelled. "Just three in my whole life, for missing a couple of stop signs and failing to use a turn signal. And I was polite and professional."

"Were you at fault?"

She squirmed in her seat. He would ask that. "Yes."

"As I said before, I rest my case."

"I never did anything to try and influence those officers."

He spared her a quick look. "You didn't have to. I was a cop for a long time. Trust me, we can be influenced by a pretty face—especially when the face is polite."

He'd called her pretty.

That was unexpected.

She sat back, trying to figure out how to respond to the backhanded compliment.

Fortunately, given Starfish Bay's tiny main street, she didn't have to worry about it. Thirty seconds later, Clint was pulling into Jaz's parking lot.

"Sit tight and I'll get your door."

She didn't argue as he set the brake and exited the truck. Instead, she did her best to switch gears and psych herself up for what was certain to be an interesting dining experience.

Clint opened her door, waited while she slid out, then took her arm as they walked toward the entrance. She was so distracted by his touch she almost didn't notice the Harley in front of the building, or the skull and crossbones spray-painted on the walls.

Almost.

The inside was worse. Twin pool tables greeted her, unused at the moment. The walls were lined with all kinds of weird memorabilia, from Grateful Dead posters to skulls with rhinestones in the eye sockets.

Oh, brother.

Clint breezed past all of that and led her to the back half of the building, where bar-height tables and stools were clustered in front of a large range and grill.

A tall man in a tight T-shirt, with longish, gray-streaked black hair and some formidable tattoos, turned from the grill as they approached.

"Hey, Clint. You're here early. You must have come right from church."

"Close. I only stopped at home long enough to change."

"I barely got here in time to open the place myself. Our pastor was on the long-winded side today. And who is this pretty little lady?"

Clint drew her forward. "Meet Kristen Andrews. She's the concierge and event planner at the inn. Kristen, this is Jaz."

The man wiped his right palm on his worn jeans and extended his hand, giving her a hearty shake. "Nice to meet you. I wasn't able to make the open house, but I expect this place is a hundred and eighty from your usual turf."

"It's very…unique."

The man guffawed. "Scary, you mean. But the truth is, we're a family restaurant. All this stuff—" he swept his hand around the interior "—is for show. It's everybody's worst image of what a biker bar should be. Over the top, you know? But hey…it brings people in. That and the food. Did Clint tell you we have amazing burgers?"

"Yes. Pizza, too."

"On your first trip, have a burger—unless you two are just paying a social call and saving lunch for another day?"

Clint deferred to her, and Kristen realized he was giving her an option to change her mind, now that she'd seen the place from the inside.

The door jingled behind them, and she glanced over her shoulder. An older couple entered, with what appeared to be grandkids in tow.

"Be with you in a sec, Hank," Jaz called. "You and Marian and the kids find a table."

Okay. Those people looked normal. They'd also brought children here. And Jaz went to church. Those pluses helped offset the decor.

"We came for lunch." She smiled at Jaz.

"All right, then." He gave her a flash of his teeth. "Menus are on the tables. You can't go wrong with any of the burgers, but my personal favorite is the cheddar and bacon. My seasoned fries are also awesome. I'll be over to get your order in a minute."

He took off for the couple with the two children, and Clint gestured to one of the tables near the wall. "That okay?"

"Fine."

He followed her over, and once seated, he held out a menu.

Smiling, she waved it aside. "I'm going with Jaz's recommendation."

"Smart choice." He set his own menu back in the holder, too. "So everything set at the inn for the opening on Friday? The place seemed to be running smoothly yesterday at the open house."

She rolled her eyes. "You weren't privy to the behind-the-scenes chaos, multiplied exponentially by Louis Mattson's presence. But I've been on hand for openings before, and despite the mayhem, we'll be fine. We only book half the rooms for the first week to give the staff a chance to settle in and get comfortable."

Jaz joined them. "What'll it be today, folks?"

"We're both going with your recommendation. And we'll share a large order of fries." Clint turned to her. "What would you like to drink?"

She smiled at Jaz. "Whatever white soda you have is fine."

"Same for me," Clint seconded.

"Got it. The grill's all fired up. It won't be long." Jaz leaned sideways to wave at some new arrivals, then detoured toward the cooking area.

"Interesting place." Kristen studied a framed collage of motorcycle license plates on a nearby wall.

Clint chuckled. "Yeah. And more than a little off-putting for the uninitiated. As is Jaz. He likes to tell the story about his appearance at the town council meeting to apply for a permit. They almost didn't give it to him, based purely on his appearance. But he's turned out to be one of the town's leading citizens—and a devout Christian, to boot."

"I caught his reference about going to church this morning. Not what you'd expect from someone who looks like him."

"Like I said yesterday at the party, looks can be deceiving."

An odd undercurrent in his voice piqued her interest, but he continued without giving her a chance to analyze it.

"I know you said you're not a church-goer, but if you change your mind, my congregation would be happy to welcome you. We have a great pastor, too."

She managed a smile. "Thanks, but if I ever want to talk with the Lord, I can always pop over to Starfish Bay Chapel right on the inn grounds."

"Have you been inside yet?"

"Of course. I've explored every inch of the property, public and private, and we've already booked a few wedding parties. The chapel is a perfect spot for a small, intimate ceremony. Very contemplative."

"I know. Lindsey at the Mercantile and her husband were married there last spring. It was the first building on the site that was completed, at Mattson's orders. Scott Walsh, the foreman on the inn project, married another Starfish Bay resident there last Christmas. Do you do a lot of wedding planning for guests?"

Too much.

That was the one part of her job she didn't enjoy. Celebrating other people's happy endings always left her feeling melancholy.

But she modified her answer for her companion. "Enough."

He gave her one of those keen looks that delved a bit too deep and made her squirm. "Bridezilla problems?"

"Not usually."

"But…?"

"But what?"

"I get the feeling that isn't your favorite part of the job."

The man was much too sharp.

"A little romantic happy-ending stuff goes a long way."

Jaz chose that moment to deliver their

drinks and fries. Perfect timing, considering Clint's speculative expression.

"I'll be back shortly with those burgers, but go ahead and dig into these." He set the basket of golden potatoes between them. "They're just out of the fryer."

As he returned to the cooking area, Kristen slid from her stool. "Would you excuse me for a minute? I'd like to wash my hands."

"Of course." Clint stood, too, and indicated the far corner of the building. "Be prepared. The theme carries over in the restrooms, too."

"Thanks for the warning."

She took off in the direction he'd indicated. No matter what awaited her in the ladies' room, she could handle it far better than a discussion about romance. If she was lucky, he'd forget all about the topic by the time she got back and they could move on to a more innocuous subject.

Unfortunately, he struck her as the kind of guy who had a long memory—and a lot of determination.

* * *

Clint watched Kristen edge around a polished Harley with a pirate-hat-wearing skeleton in the driver's seat, then fished a fry out of the basket Jaz had left on the table.

What kind of woman didn't like happy endings and brides and romantic stuff?

One who'd been burned.

What other explanation could there be?

He dipped the fry in ketchup and popped it in his mouth. Was Kristen divorced? Had she been dumped by a significant other? Or had some guy hurt her in another way?

His blood pressure edged up a few notches, and he frowned. What was that all about? He hardly knew his new tenant. Yet that reaction had felt a lot like his protective instincts kicking in.

Could be just basic human empathy, though. He hated injustice. That was one of the reasons he'd become a cop. But whatever her romantic history, the right guy should be able to fix the damage. Patience and love and kindness could heal a lot of hurt.

Her antipathy to religion bothered him more. That was a bigger stumbling block to...

Clint stopped chewing.

To what?

"Here you go." Jaz set two huge burgers on the table and scanned the room. "I didn't scare the little lady off, did I?"

"No. She went to wash her hands."

Jaz snickered. "Can't say I blame her. Happens to a lot of people first time they get a load of this place." He gave Clint a speculative look. "You know, guys who bring women in here are usually either trying to end a relationship or test out the potential. Sort of a trial by fire. How come I think you're doing the latter?"

Striving for a casual tone, Clint dipped another fry in ketchup. "I have no idea." In his peripheral vision, Kristen came into view and he transferred his attention to her. Man, she looked great today in that soft sweater that matched the jade hue of her eyes, with her hair swinging around her face.

"I do. Because when she's in sight, you can't take your eyes off of her. Not that I blame you. She's a looker."

Yeah, she was.

Kristen slipped back onto her seat and inspected the burgers. "Those look fabulous."

"Dig in. I hope you're not disappointed—especially since you're the first date Clint's ever brought here." Jaz smirked at him as he addressed Kristen.

She shot him a startled glance.

Thanks a lot, Jaz.

He fought back a flush as Kristen cleared her throat. "This isn't a date. I mentioned to Clint at the open house yesterday that I was hoping to find some other dining options for inn guests. He suggested your place and offered to bring me today for lunch."

"Is that right? Well, I'm not certain the kind of people who'll be staying at the inn will appreciate our ambience, but any adventurous types who take the chance will be welcome. And you two enjoy your lunch anyway, even if it's business." From behind Kristen, Jaz gave him a thumbs-up before crossing the room to take the order from some new arrivals.

If Kristen was embarrassed by the reference to a date, she gave no indication. She'd already cut her burger in half and taken an enormous bite.

He followed her lead.

"Okay." She swallowed the first mouthful and took a sip of soda. "You weren't exaggerating. This is the best burger I ever ate." She took another large bite.

The tension in his shoulders eased. "I'm glad you like it."

"I'm surprised, though."

"About what?" He took another bite himself.

"That you've never brought a date here. It would be memorable. And there's certainly a lot of conversation starters. Like that infinity-tunnel hall with all those weird lights that leads to the restrooms."

Chewing his burger, Clint was glad he had an excuse to delay answering. He could respond to her comment about the decor. Or he could get more personal and talk about her dating remark. It all depended on what kind of potential he saw for the two of them. Jaz had been right in his assessment of why a guy would bring a woman here.

He swallowed the bite of burger and made his decision. "I haven't brought a date here because I don't date much."

She paused with the burger halfway to her mouth. "Why not?" The instant she asked the question, color flooded her cheeks. "Sorry. None of my business." She took another bite and made a project out of selecting a fry.

"I don't mind answering. For a long time I wasn't in the market. Besides, I haven't met anyone out here I wanted to date."

She chewed on her fry and watched him. "I don't suppose Starfish Bay has a huge number of eligible women."

"Some. But I'm also looking for a woman who shares my faith."

"Ah." She continued to eat her burger, displaying a much heartier appetite than he'd expected. Lisa had always nibbled at her food and complained about her weight, even though she'd been model thin.

When the silence between them lengthened, he realized Kristen wasn't going to add anything to that comment. So he cautiously picked up the thread.

"You mentioned once you weren't a churchgoer. Have you ever been, if you don't mind me asking?"

"Yes." She wove a fry through the ketchup, faint creases marring her brow. "My family was very faith-centered. Sunday services and regular prayer were part of our life."

"So what happened?"

She jabbed the fry in the ketchup and pulled it out. "I fell away after I went to college. It happens to a lot of kids." She bit into the fry and chewed. "Look, I'm not sure what prompted this discussion, but if, by chance, you have any interest in me, I'm not—to use your phrase—in the market. It's nothing personal. You seem like a nice guy, but I'm not looking for a relationship. Besides, since God and I parted company years ago and I don't anticipate a reunion in the foreseeable future, it wouldn't work anyway. Now tell me more about your job as a ranger. What's the most interesting thing that's happened to you?"

The lady wanted to change the subject.

He wanted to know more.

Why wasn't she in the market for a relationship? And why had her faith lapsed? The going-away-to-college explanation didn't ring true.

But she wasn't going to tell him anything else today. He could tell that from the grip she had on her burger and the firm set of her chin.

So he went along with her change of subject. Told her some stories. Listened as she reciprocated with a few hilarious tales about her experiences as a concierge.

Found himself laughing and relaxing and having the best time he'd had in years.

All of which only made him want to get to know her better.

When Jaz delivered the bill, he pulled out his wallet and started to riffle through the plastic credit-card holders.

"No. I'll get this. I can expense it." She touched his hand with her fingertips, the polished crimson nails contrasting with her fair skin.

A spurt of adrenaline hiked up his pulse, and the wallet slipped from his fingers, falling onto the table. It opened to the plastic sleeve holding Lisa's photo.

The one he should have taken out long ago.

Kristen's gaze fell on it for a brief instant before he could snatch it back.

Without comment, she withdrew her hand and rummaged around in her purse.

"I'd say you liked your lunch." Jaz beamed at their empty plates.

"It was fabulous." Kristen withdrew her

own card and handed it over. "I'll definitely be sending some guests your way."

"More business is always welcome. I'll get your receipt."

As Jaz walked toward the cooking area, Kristen gave Clint a smile that seemed a tad forced. "Thanks for suggesting this. I have to admit, without your prompt I might never have ventured in here."

"To be honest, I was in town for six months before I gave it a try. Lindsey finally goaded me into it."

His brief account of his first foot-dragging visit brought a smile to her lips.

"Here you go." Jaz slid the receipt in front of Kristen. She signed it and handed it back. "You two come back again, okay? Next visit you'll have to try my rattlesnake pizza." As Kristen's eyes widened, he laughed. "Gotcha."

She laughed. "Rattlesnake pizza here wouldn't surprise me, though."

"Yeah. It would fit. And it might be fun to try. But for now, the three-meat, three-cheese with mushrooms and green peppers is my personal favorite. Have Clint bring you back for another research trip so you can try that, too." He winked at her.

Her cheeks pinkened and she slid to her feet. "I'll put that on the list for my next visit. Ready?" She turned to Clint.

"All set. Thanks, Jaz. See you soon."

He took her arm as they wove through the diners and the pool tables, where high-spirited games were now under way between two older gents at one table and some teens at another. She didn't protest his proprietary gesture, but once outside she gently extricated herself from his grip as they walked toward the car.

Her message was clear.

Hands off.

No romance.

Keep your distance.

He didn't have any difficulty interpreting her subtle communication.

But as he drove the short distance back to his house and they parted in his driveway, he was having difficulty reconciling her message with his sudden yearning to get to know his new tenant a whole lot better.

A yearning that he had a sinking feeling was likely to remain unfulfilled—despite the upbeat platitude about dreams coming true on the place mats at the Orchid Café.

Chapter Seven

Opening day had been a resounding success.

But it had also been long, long, long. Kristen had been on the run from the instant she stepped inside the inn until the instant she left twelve hours later.

And as she wearily climbed the stairs to her apartment on Friday night, she knew the grueling pace wasn't going to let up during the long Memorial Day weekend just beginning. Holidays were always busy at Mattson resorts, more so when an inn was just opening. Not only did you have to deal with guest requests, you also had to keep a sharp eye on new staff as they moved into the on-the-job training phase. There were few allowances for mistakes from the discriminating guests who chose a Mattson resort.

Still, she was confident she had things under control.

Once inside her apartment, Kristen dumped her purse on the kitchen counter, filled a glass with water and dropped onto a stool. What a day. All she wanted to do was fall into bed—perhaps fully clothed. She was even tempted to let her phone messages wait until tomorrow. After all, the clock was already inching toward eleven.

No. Better to get that over with tonight. The phone had vibrated numerous times during the day, but she'd been too busy with guests to answer it. Still, there weren't likely to be any important messages. Every inn employee she'd needed to talk with on opening day had been on-site. It shouldn't take her long to check the messages.

She groped around inside her purse, pulled out the phone and scrolled through the calls. Nothing there that couldn't keep overni—

Wait.

With a flick of her finger, she backed up to a message from noon. The number wasn't familiar, but the Denver area code was.

She scrolled farther down.

There it was again. The same Denver number, three hours later.

At eight o'clock tonight, yet another Denver call, from a different number.

Feeling suddenly queasy, she played the first message back.

"Kristen, it's Connie Walters. Would you please call me as soon as possible? I have some information I need to share with you." The woman recited her number.

Connie Walters.

She hadn't spoken with the woman in more than nine years. But hearing her voice again brought back a torrent of emotions she'd thought she'd long ago put to rest.

Fear. Shame. Panic. Guilt. Desperation. Despair.

Forcing herself to continue breathing, she played back the second message from the woman.

"Kristen, it's Connie again. I need you to call me soon, please. I have an urgent matter to discuss. If you get this after hours, call my cell." She recited a number.

It matched the ID from the third and final call, made three hours ago.

Trying to rein in her panic, Kristen played back that message.

"It's Connie. No matter what time you get this, call me. If I don't hear from you tonight, I'll check with your employer tomorrow and see if they can track you down." This time the woman's tone was agitated.

Something bad had happened.

Kristen's hand started to shake.

Please, God, let Beatrice be all right!

The prayer was spontaneous, ripped from her soul. Even if she was too ashamed to approach God and ask forgiveness for herself, she wasn't above praying for Beatrice.

The daughter she'd never met.

The daughter she'd given away.

The daughter whose life she followed through Connie at Babes in Arms Adoption Agency.

Heart pounding, she punched in the number as fast as her unsteady fingers would allow.

The woman answered on the first ring.

"It's Kristen. What's wrong?"

"Kristen! Thank God you called!"

She clenched the phone. Tried to brace herself. "Did something happen to Beatrice?"

"No. She's fine—physically, anyway. But her adoptive parents were killed in a small commuter-plane crash last night. Their attorney contacted us today. They arranged to have their assets put in a trust for Beatrice, but they left instructions for you to be notified if anything ever happened to them. They didn't have any siblings, and both sets of grandparents are gone, since they adopted at an older age. They knew you'd followed Beatrice's life, and they wanted you to have the chance to take her back."

Waves of shock ricocheted through Kristen as she tried to absorb the news. "Take her back?"

"It's a second chance, Kristen. I know how you agonized over the decision at the time, and how you've kept up with her ever since. Not many people get the opportunity to revisit a choice like that."

"W-where is she now?" Kristen massaged her forehead and stared at the blank wall across from her.

"With a friend's family. Her parents were taking a weekend trip for their twentieth anniversary. It was the first time they'd ever left her alone with anyone, but she can't stay there long. That's why I need an answer from you quickly."

"What happens if…if I don't take her?"

"She'll be put into foster care. The adoptive parents only had distant cousins, and they have no interest in taking her. The attorney asked us to check with you and see if it was all right to release your contact information to him."

"Does Beatrice…know about me?"

"She knows she's adopted. That's all. I talked with her friend's mother today. The woman told me she's very traumatized, as you might expect." There was a moment of silence on the line. "I don't mean to rush you, but the authorities will be moving on this fast. I'm not saying you couldn't get her back later if you chose to, but it would minimize her distress to go straight to you and skip the foster-care step, if that's your choice."

Kristen sucked in a deep breath, rested her elbow on the counter and propped her head in her hand. A child would completely disrupt her life. She hadn't even settled into her new job or home yet. How would she deal with day-care arrangements? How would she console a grieving little girl? What did she know about raising a child? What would she tell people—especially her family—about this child she'd never acknowledged to anyone but God and the father, who'd been more than happy to sign away any parental rights?

But those were some of the very excuses she'd used nine years ago to justify abdicating her responsibility.

Her stomach twisted into a knot.

"Kristen?"

"Yes. I'm still here."

"I'm sorry to dump this on you. I know how much of a shock it must be."

No kidding.

She stood and began to pace in the tiny galley kitchen. "Look, I've just put in a very long day. I'm exhausted and not thinking very clearly. I need to digest this overnight. Can I call you first thing tomorrow?"

"Of course. As we discussed before the adoption, you need to be comfortable with whatever you decide. If you don't want Beatrice, don't take her. In the end, that could be more damaging than having her go to foster care. Children can sense if they're not wanted—and it's worse if they're not wanted by a family member. Keep her best interests at heart now, as you did then."

Except she hadn't kept Beatrice's best interests at heart back then. She'd selfishly given her own interests top priority.

"I'll get back to you by eight o'clock your time. And thank you for calling, Connie."

As they rang off, Kristen pushed the end button and set the phone on the counter, sinking back onto the stool as numbness robbed the strength from her legs.

What on earth was she supposed to do?

Or maybe the real question was, what in heaven was she supposed to do? Because while she might have told Clint her faith had lapsed, that wasn't quite accurate. She'd never stopped believing in God. She'd just stopped believing she was worthy of His love.

But He was still there. Watching over her, she hoped, as she wrestled with this unexpected opportunity to not only find redemption, but to have the chance to be part of all those special moments she'd only participated in through the photos

Beatrice's adoptive parents had passed on to her through the agency.

Rising again, she trudged toward the bathroom, ticking off her plan for the evening. First, take a long, hot shower. Second, look through the album of photos of her daughter that she'd collected through the years. Third, drink a lot of coffee. And finally, pray very hard.

There would be no sleep this night. She'd need every minute until she called Connie back to wrestle with her decision.

Because second chances were a rare gift.

And she didn't want to blow this one by making another mistake.

Something was wrong.

Clint lay on his back, staring at the ceiling in his bedroom, listening to Kristen pace.

She'd been at it since he'd gone to bed at eleven o'clock—two long hours.

Had things gone awry on opening day?

Or was the reason for her restlessness more serious than work-related problems?

The pacing continued as the minutes ticked by. One-fifteen. One-thirty. One forty-five.

When the digital clock on his nightstand rolled to two, he threw back the covers, pulled on jeans and a sweatshirt and shoved his feet into his shoes. Kristen would no doubt consider such a late-night call an intrusion, but how could he lie here and listen to her obvious agitation without offering to help? If she shut the door in his face, so be it. At least he could console himself that he'd tried.

He exited through the front door, circled the house in the chilly night air and climbed the steps toward her apartment. As he approached the landing, he could see her pacing shadow on the drawn shades. When he reached the top, the motion detector activated the light above the door.

The shadow froze.

He moved closer to the door. "Kristen? It's Clint."

The shadow remained motionless.

Had his voice not carried through the

thick wood? Or had she chosen to ignore him?

As he debated his next move, the shadow melted away. A few seconds later, he heard her sliding the lock open. Then she cracked the door. Her face was too dim to read, but the distinct aroma of freshly brewed coffee wafted out.

"Sorry to bother you in the middle of the night, but I heard you walking around and wondered if everything was okay."

"Yes. Fine. I apologize if I kept you awake."

She was lying. Her words were shaky, and her grip on the edge of the door was cutting off the flow of blood to her knuckles, turning them white.

He gentled his tone. "I wasn't expressing a complaint, but a concern."

"I appreciate that." The last word broke, and she cleared her throat. "But I'm fine."

Get out of here, Nolan. She doesn't want you.

"As long as I made the trip, would you mind sharing a cup of that coffee I smell?

Since I'm awake anyway." So much for walking away. The words were out before he could stop them.

She hesitated for a heartbeat, then pulled the door open and gestured him in.

Without giving her a chance for second thoughts, he crossed the threshold—and got his first clear look at her.

Gone was the polished, sophisticated, in-control concierge.

In her place was a distraught woman dressed in an old, faded sweatsuit, her face scrubbed clean of makeup, her eyes haunted.

It took every ounce of his willpower not to follow his instincts and pull her close for a comforting hug.

"Do you take cream or sugar?"

Her question registered somewhere in the back of his mind as she rounded the counter. "Black is fine."

She picked up the pot—too soon. The coffee was still brewing. She let out a startled yelp and tried to shove the pot back into position, but some of the steaming liquid splattered onto the back of her hand.

At her cry of pain, he was beside her in an instant. With one hand, he removed the pot from her fingers. With the other, he leaned over and turned on the cold-water tap.

"Put your hand under there while I get some ice."

After repositioning the pot, he yanked open the freezer compartment, scooped up a handful of cubes and wrapped them in the dish towel lying on the sink. He twisted the ends and pressed it against the angry red mark already appearing on her hand.

She regarded his makeshift ice pack dully, as if she was in shock—pale, trembling and out of it.

Clint's pulse ratcheted up. Whatever had put her in this catatonic state had to be bad.

Very bad.

"Why don't you go sit in the living room for a minute and let the ice work on that burn?"

He started to guide her around the counter, but she held back. When he looked at her, he saw a fat tear forming on the brim of one eye. In a moment it would spill over and trail down her cheek.

Her quick swipe told him she knew it was there, too.

"Pour yourself a cup of coffee while I… uh… I'll be back in a minute."

With that, she fled out of the kitchen, across the living room and down the hall. He heard the sound of a door closing. A tap was turned on.

But it couldn't muffle the sound of choked sobs, as she'd obviously hoped it would.

What in the world was going on?

Clint combed his fingers through his hair. What could have happened to make a strong, survivor type like Kristen crumble? The answer eluded him. But he didn't intend to leave until he got some clarity or she was a lot calmer. Preferably both.

He filled a mug with coffee, then walked into the living room. An open photo album on the coffee table—the only personal item in the room—caught his eye, and he walked over to it.

Huh.

Every single shot featured the same blond-haired little girl, age four or five, smiling into the camera. In one photo, she was sitting behind a birthday cake, the lit candles illuminating her megawatt grin. In another, she was holding a worn, obviously well-loved Raggedy Ann doll. A third featured her dressed up as Cinderella. A Halloween shot, perhaps.

He lifted the corners of a few other pages and checked them out. Same little girl in every picture, at different ages.

Who was she?

And why did Kristen have all these pictures of her?

As he puzzled over that, a hand reached into his field of vision and closed the book.

He hadn't even heard his tenant return.

Praying she wouldn't throw him out for prying into material she clearly considered private, he shifted toward her. She still had the ice pressed to the back of her hand, but now her eyes were pink and puffy, too.

"I appreciate you coming up to check on me, but I really am fine."

She sounded more in control. Somehow she'd managed to pick up the pieces and put herself together again, at least for the moment. No way was she going to admit she'd been crying—or tell him who the little girl was.

Her message was clear: go home.

Instead, he sat on the couch.

Fingers clenched around the ice pack, she sent him a dismayed look. "I was thinking about going to bed."

He took a sip of coffee, buying himself a few seconds to plan his strategy. "You know, when problems seem overwhelming, sometimes it helps to bounce them off someone."

"I'm not overwhelmed."

"You could have fooled me." He watched her, daring her to deny it.

She caved faster than he'd expected.

"Okay, I'm dealing with a…difficult situation. But I'll figure it out."

"If you don't want to talk to me, is there someone else you can call? Your mother, brother, a friend?"

The echo of despair in her eyes was impossible to miss. "No. I'll handle it on my own. But I appreciate that you cared enough to stop by." Once more, tears welled in her eyes. Once more, she brushed them away—and tried without much success to adopt a teasing tone. "I didn't realize you took your job as a landlord so seriously."

"I'm not here tonight as a landlord. Why don't you put me in the friend category?"

"No." She gave a jerky shake of her head, a flicker of…panic?…tightening her features. "I don't want to make any friends. It's easier to move on if you don't have any ties."

"It's also lonelier."

"I'm used to it. My job fills in the gaps."

She wasn't going to share anything with him. Not tonight. But at least he'd planted the seed for confidences, let her know he was available if she wanted to talk. That was the best he could do for now.

Draining his cup, he rose and walked toward the kitchen. "I don't want to overstay my welcome. If I can help in any way, though, don't hesitate to call."

She trailed after him. "There is one thing."

He rinsed his cup, set it in the sink and swiveled toward her. "Name it."

"I may be gone for a few days. If that happens, I'd appreciate it if you'd keep my mail for me."

It was on the tip of his tongue to ask her where she was going.

He bit the question back.

"Sure."

At the door, though, he stopped and turned back. "I know you said you'd left your faith behind, but it might not hurt to have a chat with the Lord. He's a great listener."

Her lips lifted in a shaky smile that held no mirth. "Believe it or not, I've been bending His ear for the past five hours. But thanks for the advice."

With a nod, he exited and pulled the door shut behind him. A few seconds later, as he heard the lock slide back into place, he was still thinking about her last admission.

Kristen was praying.

Given her earlier comments about her faith, that fact alone told him she was in desperate need of help.

And as he descended the stairs, he added his voice to hers.

Because he had a feeling whatever problem she faced, she could use all the prayers she could get.

Chapter Eight

Clint tightened his grip on the ax. Lifted it. Swung. It landed with a satisfying thud in the base of a half-dead spruce tree smack in the middle of the spot planned for the last bench along the interpretive trail on The Point.

He yanked it out, then dipped his head to wipe his brow on the sleeve of his T-shirt. There were a lot of less taxing ways to spend a Sunday afternoon. He could take a walk on Agate Beach. Read the latest thriller he'd bought on his last trip to Eureka. Stop in for coffee and conversation at the Orchid. After all, the contractor who was doing the bulk of the work on the trail that led through the woods and along the edge of the headland toward the chapel had offered to clear this final niche.

But thanks to Kristen, he needed this physical labor.

He took another swing, trying to expel the restless energy that had kept sleep at bay since their unsettling tête-à-tête in the wee hours of Saturday morning. It had taken him a long while to fall back asleep after he'd returned to his room, but at last he'd crashed. Only the engine of her car starting at eight-fifteen had roused him. He'd vaulted out of bed just in time to see her taillights disappear down his driveway. She'd still been gone when he'd gotten home later in the day after his shift at the park, but he'd heard her come in later.

Early this morning, he'd again heard her car start. And the note she'd taped to the front door, confirming she'd left for a few days, had been woefully lacking in details. All he'd been able to conclude from the half gallon of milk she'd deposited beside his door and her request that he fill the bowl on her landing once a day was that she'd adopted the stray kitten he'd seen hanging around the place for the past week or two.

But the biggest question of all had been left unanswered.

Why would a dedicated employee walk away from the inn on opening weekend? A holiday weekend, to boot.

Frustrated, he continued to whack at the tree trunk as needles rained down on him. Though he tried to shake them off, they stuck to his shirt, refusing to relinquish their hold.

Sort of like thoughts of Kristen.

As he lifted the ax again, his cell began to vibrate. He stopped midswing to grab it out of his pocket, his pulse accelerating. Maybe it was her. Maybe she'd decided to share a few more details about the crisis that had triggered her unexpected trip.

A quick check of the LED display dashed those hopes, however. But it was a welcome call nonetheless.

He pressed the talk button and put the

phone to his ear, turning to gaze at the distant vista of the sea. It was calm and placid on this clear day, in direct contrast to his emotions.

"Hi, Dad." He rested the head of the ax on the ground and propped a shoulder against the tree trunk. "How are things?"

"Can't complain. Remember how I was afraid I'd be bored after I retired last year?" A snort came over the line. "What a laugh. Those grandkids keep me on the go. I spent the whole afternoon at the beach with them yesterday. Slept like a log last night."

Clint smiled as he pictured his sister's children. Last time he'd seen them, six-year-old Jeremy had been into Spider-Man and eight-year-old Lauren had been captivated by fairy-tale princesses. Of course, the image in his mind was almost a year old, and kids changed fast at that age.

"I'll be glad to see you all when you come out in July."

"We'll be glad to see you, too. The kids

were disappointed you didn't visit us for Christmas."

His dad had been, too. He'd heard it in the man's voice when he'd called last December to send his regrets. But to his father's credit, the older man had never criticized any of his choices.

Even the bad ones.

"I may come back this year."

"We'd all like that. And maybe it's time." A charged moment of silence put Clint on alert. "People move on, you know. Things change."

After thirty-four years, he'd learned to recognize the subtle shifts in his father's inflection. His dad had news. "Anything in particular?"

"As a matter of fact, I had a call from Lisa yesterday."

Clint's breath hitched, but he did his best to maintain a conversational tone. "That's a surprise. What did she want?"

"She asked me to pass the word to you that she's getting married to a fellow attorney."

The world went silent, as if a clear bubble had been dropped over him. The birds stopped singing, the waves stopped crashing, the seals on the rock below stopped barking as his father's words echoed in his mind.

He'd assumed this would happen someday. Lisa was young, attractive, accomplished. A broken engagement might have slowed her up, but it wouldn't stop her from creating the life she wanted. A life that included career, husband and kids—perhaps in that order.

Funny. He'd tried to prepare himself for this moment, had assumed he'd be devastated when he finally got the news.

But he wasn't.

And he suspected a certain concierge could take a lot of the credit for that.

"You okay, son?"

At the concern in his father's tone, he refocused on the conversation. "Yeah. I'm fine. Really. Lisa and I were over three years ago. I knew there was no chance of a reconciliation." Not after the hateful words she'd flung at him that night at the hospital—though they'd been no worse than the ones he'd heaped on himself. He'd deserved every bit of censure she'd directed at him.

"Well, she thought it was only right to let you know, since the two of you were engaged and all. She also asked me for your address. She wants to write you a letter. I told her I'd have to check with you."

"That's not necessary. I'm over it."

"Maybe it's necessary for her."

Clint's first inclination was still to say no. But if Lisa wanted to do this, if it helped give her closure, he ought to honor her request. It was the least he could do.

"Fine. You can give her my address."

"Okay. I'll pass it on. So how's everything out there? Meet any interesting people?"

Clint did the translation and answered the implied question. "Everything's fine. And no, I'm not dating anyone."

"Isn't it about time you did, if you're really over it?"

Checkmate for his dad.

"I'll get around to it one of these days."

The sound of a sigh came over the line. "I worry about you, you know. A man like you ought to have a passel of kids running around. But I expect the pickings are slim in Starfish Bay. That's one of the downsides of small towns."

"I don't know. New people show up every day, especially with the inn open now."

"That's a plus, I'll grant you. And you sure did pick a pretty place to settle. By the way, the kids are looking forward to another trip to Agate Beach when we come out."

"I'll add that to our agenda. Give my love to everyone, okay?"

"Will do. And you take care of yourself. Go meet some of those new people at the inn."

His father had a one-track mind.

"I'll think about it. Talk to you soon, Dad."

Clint rang off, glad he'd resisted the

temptation to mention Kristen. His father would be all over that news, and it was too soon to raise his dad's expectations.

Or his own.

Before he let himself get carried away about any possibilities with the new concierge, he needed to get to know her a whole lot better. And until she felt comfortable sharing personal information—like the reasons why she'd written off romance, didn't want friends and took mysterious trips—that wasn't likely to happen.

Choking down a few more of her French fries, Kristen checked out her daughter's almost-untouched meal. Beatrice had taken only one small bite of the burger, nibbled at a couple of fries and sipped a half inch of milk, all the while clutching her Raggedy Ann doll.

Nor had she done much better this morning before they'd boarded their flight in Denver. Her breakfast had consisted of one piece of bacon and a glass of orange juice. And she hadn't eaten a thing on the plane, even though Kristen had stocked her shoulder bag with cookies and peanut butter crackers and potato chips—all the bad stuff kids were supposed to like.

But in light of the past few traumatic days, her daughter's lack of appetite was no surprise. The poor child had lost the only parents she'd ever known; sat through the heartrending ritual of the private memorial service; watched as the contents of her home were labeled for shipment to the West Coast, storage or charity; and was now being whisked across the country to a place she'd never been with a mother she didn't know.

Still, she had to eat. Since they'd met on Sunday afternoon three days ago, she'd barely ingested the equivalent of one full meal a day. At this rate, she'd be malnourished in a week.

A tsunami of panic crashed over Kristen, and she took a sip of her soft drink, trying to wash the taste of fear from her mouth. She wasn't equipped to handle a traumatized child. She had no idea how to…

"I need to use the bathroom."

Her hand jerked, rattling the ice in her cup. Her daughter had spoken so seldom, and usually in monosyllables, that she wasn't yet accustomed to her soft, musical voice.

"Okay." She looked around the fast-food place and spotted the sign. "I'll leave my jacket here so people know we're coming back."

"We don't have to if you don't want. I'm finished."

Hesitating, Kristen once more examined her daughter's uneaten meal. Should she pressure her to take a few more bites? Or use the trip home to try to ferret out what foods her daughter liked, then grab them at the Mercantile and encourage her to eat once she'd settled in?

"Are you sure you don't want any more?"

Beatrice gave her a solemn nod.

"Okay." Decision made, she gathered up the food, stuffed it all back in the bag and slid out of the booth. Beatrice followed her, holding her cup and the doll. "Why don't you drink some more milk during the drive?"

Again, the girl nodded.

Ten minutes later, buckled into her seat, Beatrice sipped at her milk and held her doll close as they started the drive north on 101.

The car was silent as Kristen tried to think of some topic that would engage the child. She needed to open the lines of communication. Establish a connection that would…

"How come you gave me away when I was a baby?"

At the soft, unexpected question, Kristen's heart stuttered and the air whooshed out of her lungs. She'd known this issue would come up sooner or later, but she'd been praying for later. With all the trauma of the past few days, she hadn't had a moment to think about how to handle issues like this.

Beatrice deserved an answer, however.

She'd have to wing it.

"I…uh…was very young. I didn't think

I would be able to take care of you very well."

That was true enough—as far as it went.

"Didn't my real daddy want me, either?"

God, I could use some help here! Please!

"He was very young, too. It's better if a little boy or girl is raised by a couple who's going to stay together and has a nice home where they can all live."

"Doesn't my real daddy live with you?"

Her palms started to sweat.

"No, honey. I haven't seen him in a very long time. Not since before you were born. I don't know where he lives now."

She had to change the subject. Fast. She wasn't prepared for this discussion, and she could do more harm than good if it continued.

"I liked where you lived, though. It's a very pretty house. And the lady and man who adopted you were very nice, weren't they?"

As Kristen glanced over, Beatrice's chin quivered. A tear rolled down the child's cheek, and she buried her face in her doll. "Yes." The word came out muffled. Wretched. "I loved my mommy and daddy—and I hate God for taking them away from me! Why would He do that?"

Her thin shoulders began to shake, and Kristen's throat tightened. "I don't know, honey, but God always has reasons. Maybe He wanted the two of us to be together." She knew it was a lame response the instant the words left her mouth. Worse than lame.

"I'd rather be with my mommy and daddy! You'll never be my mommy!"

The vehement declaration was like a punch in the gut.

And she deserved it.

But they were stuck with each other now. She'd made that commitment, and she wasn't backing down—even if her daughter's sudden burst of antipathy didn't bode well for a smooth transition for either of them.

Kristen removed one hand from the wheel and wiped her slippery palm on her slacks. She'd probably made a mistake by turning down her mother's offer to take some vacation from her job and come out for a couple of weeks. She'd thought it would be better for her and Beatrice to have some one-on-one time together before any other new players were introduced.

From all indications, however, she was going to need every bit of help she could get.

The sun glinted off the water to her left, and she ventured a quick look at the placid sea, willing some of the calm to seep into her soul. Much as she'd dreaded the conversation with her mother, their heart-to-heart had turned out to be the sole bright spot in her life since Connie had dropped her bombshell Friday night.

Funny. All these years she'd been afraid to admit what she'd done, afraid to face her mom's disappointment. Yet once her mother had absorbed the news, she'd been totally supportive—making Kristen wonder why she'd waited so long to share the secret that had burdened her soul, and reminding her again of what a terrible mistake she'd made nine years ago when she'd let pride and fear stop her from doing the right thing.

Quiet sobs from the passenger seat sliced through her heart, and once more she looked over at Beatrice. The little girl had wedged herself into the corner, as far away as possible from the mother she didn't want.

Kristen longed to comfort her. To pull her close and hold her and promise her everything would be okay. She'd stop the car and do that if she thought it would help, but she doubted Beatrice would welcome such a gesture.

Everything *would* be okay, though. For in her long night of prayer and soul-searching, interrupted only by the unexpected visit from Clint, she'd vowed that this time there would be no mistakes. She was going to win the affection of the daughter whose life until now had unfolded before her only in photos. She was going to be the mother she should have been all along. She was going to make things right.

Whatever it took.

Kristen was back.

As Clint swung into his driveway and spotted her car, his growing fear that she might never return evaporated. He'd even called the inn yesterday, asking for her. One of the assistant concierges had told him she was expected back later in the week, but that hadn't reassured him.

The presence of her car, however, did.

Still, he wanted to see her in person. *Needed* to see her—and the sooner the better. He wouldn't even bother changing out of his uniform first.

Once past her car, he parked, hurried inside and grabbed her few pieces of mail off the hall table. While their delivery could wait until tomorrow, he couldn't—even if that meant interrupting her dinner.

Back outside, he took the steps two at a time. Once on the landing, he paused outside her door to let his pulse slow, then knocked.

No response.

He knocked again.

The door cracked two inches.

But no one was there.

At a sudden, sharp intake of breath he dropped his gaze. A little girl, who looked like an older version of the child in the photo album he'd seen on Kristen's coffee table, stood half-hidden behind the door.

Before he could speak, she gave a terrified shriek and raced, sobbing, back into the apartment.

What on earth…?

He took one step over the threshold. In the recesses of the apartment, a door slammed, cutting off the sobs. Two seconds later, another door opened.

"Kristen?"

At his puzzled call, she poked her towel-wrapped head out of the hall, her eyes wide with alarm. "What happened?"

"I don't know. A little girl answered my

knock, and then she started crying and ran away."

Without a word, Kristen disappeared. He heard a door open, and the gut-wrenching sounds of the child's sobs once more echoed through the quiet apartment.

He fisted his hands on his hips. What was he supposed to do now? No one had invited him in. Yet how could he leave after seeing the flashes of fear on both female faces? He wasn't accustomed to walking away from people in need, but he didn't want to intru—

Clint frowned and sniffed. What was that smell? Was something burning?

The sudden raucous screech of the smoke alarm in the kitchen answered his question.

Spinning toward the sound, he saw black smoke seeping out around the edges of the oven door.

The burning smell intensified.

He strode toward the oven, yanked the door open—and found himself engulfed in a black haze.

Over the sound of his own coughing and the strident, ear-piercing alarm, he heard Kristen's half-hysterical comment. "I forgot all about the pizza!"

Mystery solved.

Kristen thrust some pot holders into his hand, and he grabbed the charred pizza. "Open the front door."

Eyes burning, he passed through to the landing and tossed the pizza over the railing to the grass below. Then he braced himself on the wooden banister, palms flat, drawing in lungfuls of clear air.

"Are you okay?"

At Kristen's shaky question, he turned. The towel had slipped sideways and was half off her hair. She was wearing a mismatched T-shirt and shorts, and there wasn't a speck of makeup on her face.

But what he noticed most was her pallor—and her frantic expression.

"I think I should ask *you* that question." He raised his voice, as she had, to be heard over the alarm.

"I've been better." She backed toward

the door and gestured vaguely inside. "I need to check on Beatrice. I'll be back in a few minutes, unless you don't want to wait around. Don't feel obligated." With that, she took off.

He got the message. She didn't want him to hang around.

Too bad.

Reentering, he propped the door open and waved the lingering smoke out with a dish towel until the alarm fell silent.

The muffled sobs from down the hall had ceased, but in their place he heard the murmur of voices, the words too soft to discern.

Mouth settling into a determined line, he crossed the room, planted himself next to the sliding door and waited.

Five minutes later, Kristen reappeared in the doorway that led from the hall to the living room, keeping her distance. "You didn't have to stay."

"I don't walk out on trouble."

"It's not your trouble."

"Part of it is. I don't make a habit of scaring children."

She waved a hand in dismissal. "It wasn't you. It was the uniform."

"She doesn't like park rangers?"

"Policemen." When he raised an eyebrow, she sighed and grabbed at the slipping towel. "Her parents were killed last Friday in a small plane crash, and a policeman came to speak with the friend's parents who were watching her. I guess she associates the uniform with bad news."

"Why don't you let me talk to her? I've done a fair number of programs for kids in my ranger job, and I had plenty of experience as a cop dealing with traumatized people. Including children."

A ray of hope chased some of the distress from Kristen's features. "Do you really think you can calm her down?"

"It's worth a try. Give me five minutes to change."

He crossed to the door and clattered down the steps, mulling over the task ahead. While he'd do his best to convince the little girl that not all men in uniform brought bad news, he couldn't help her cope with the tragedy that had left her parentless. That task seemed to have fallen to Kristen.

Why?

That was a question only his tenant could answer.

And this day wasn't going to end until she did.

Chapter Nine

"He's a park ranger, Beatrice. You know, like Smokey the Bear? He's not a policeman. He lives on the first floor, and he's a very nice man. He was just coming up to say hello."

Perched on the edge of her daughter's bed, Kristen had delivered three different versions of that message since Clint had left five minutes ago. But as far as she could tell, it was having zero impact. The little girl was curled into a ball, facing the wall as she clutched her doll with one hand and the strap of a backpack containing favorite items from her bedroom with the other. Her shoulders continued to tremble, though the sobs had ceased.

Kristen laid a hand on her arm. "Beatrice, honey, I..."

The girl recoiled at her touch.

Tears pricking her eyes, Kristen dropped her hand back into her lap. So much for her attempts to comfort the little girl.

Nor had her whirlwind efforts to make her daughter feel welcome been any more successful.

She scanned the room, taking in the Cinderella bedspread and the stuffed animals and the fairy princess posters. All the things she'd run around buying on Saturday, in between talking to Connie and the lawyer and the funeral home. If Beatrice had even noticed the decor, she'd given no indication.

Because no matter how hard Kristen tried, it wasn't home.

Maybe it never would be.

A knock sounded on the front door, and she pulled herself to her feet, more depressed than ever as she trudged down the hall and through the living room to answer it.

When she opened the door, Clint slipped past her. He'd changed into jeans and a T-shirt and was holding a box containing a frozen pizza.

"A replacement—for later." He slid it onto the counter. "How is she?"

"She stopped crying, but she isn't communicating."

"Where is she from?"

"Denver."

"Does she have a favorite hobby or special talent?"

He was looking for a topic that would engage her daughter. How sad that she couldn't help him out. "I don't know." She choked out the words as she led him back to the bedroom.

Clint stopped on the threshold and gave the new decor a once-over as she entered.

"Beatrice, honey, my neighbor wants to say hello. He's not in his uniform anymore. And he likes boys and girls. In fact, he takes them on hikes in the woods and teaches them all about nature." She checked with him over her shoulder, not certain she was correctly depicting his interaction with children, but he nodded. "Can you say hello to him?"

The little girl ignored her.

With an apologetic glance toward Clint, she gave a helpless shrug.

"Why don't you go ahead and dry your hair while Beatrice and I get acquainted?" Clint moved into the room, plucked the slipping towel off her head and handed it to her.

She mouthed *good luck* as she stepped around him.

Her daughter stiffened when he settled on the bed beside her. But if her landlord noticed the child's silent *go away* message, he ignored it.

"My name's Clint, Beatrice. I heard you're from Denver. Have you ever been to Rocky Mountain National Park?"

She didn't respond.

He continued as if she had. "I was there once. I liked the mountains a lot. We don't have mountains like that in the park where I work, but we have trees almost as tall. They're so big people call them giants, like the kind the Swiss Family Robinson might have lived in, or that Jack from the beanstalk story might have climbed. You have to tilt your head really far back to see the top. And some of the trunks are hollow at the bottom. You can walk inside without bending over. We have giant ferns, too. They're taller than you are. And from the beach, you can sometimes see huge whales."

As he spoke, Beatrice peeked at him over her shoulder.

Interpreting that as a positive sign, Kristen edged into the hall, keeping an eye on the duo as she reached in to grab her comb from the bathroom vanity.

"Is everything in your park big?"

Yes! He'd sparked her daughter's interest!

Clint chuckled. "Not everything. Banana slugs are on the small side."

"What's a banana slug?"

She could see only part of Clint's profile,

but she caught a glimpse of an endearing dimple in his cheek when he smiled. Why had she never noticed it before? "It's a little critter about this long." He illustrated with his two index fingers. "And it's bright yellow. It looks a lot like a tiny banana."

The tight coil of Beatrice's body loosened a bit. "Could a person live in one of those big, hollow trees?"

"I expect they could. Some of the trunks are almost as big as this room."

"That might be fun. It sounds like something from a storybook."

"It could get chilly in there at night, though. But they're a lot of fun to play in. When I take children on hikes, I always stop at some of those trees."

"I've never seen a tree that big."

"Maybe your...Kristen...will take you to see them while you're here."

The touch of animation that had brightened Beatrice's features faded. "I don't want to go with her."

The knot in Kristen's stomach tightened again. She still couldn't see Clint's face, but he had to be wondering about Beatrice's flat repudiation.

"I'm sure we can figure out a way for you to take a trip there. In the meantime, why don't we eat some of the pepperoni pizza I brought? I'll tell you some stories about the park if you have a piece."

Beatrice leaned sideways to look around him, toward the hall. Toward her. Kristen's heart sank at the animosity on her daughter's face. "Is she going to eat with us, too?"

Angling her direction, Clint shot her a quizzical glance.

"I'm not that hungry. I could…uh…unpack while you guys have the pizza."

"I might eat some, then." Beatrice sank back on the bed, out of sight.

When Clint hesitated, Kristen jumped in. She'd fast for a week if that would get some food into her daughter's stomach. "I'll put it in the oven while you two talk some more."

Before either could respond, she swiveled away and jogged toward the kitchen.

Their voices followed her, one low and deep, the other high-pitched and childlike. Beatrice had talked more in the past ten minutes than she had since Kristen had met her. If only her daughter would do the same with her.

Yet as she set out plates, napkins, drinks and finally the hot pizza, then retreated to the bathroom, she was more concerned about the coming conversation with Clint. He wasn't going to leave without some answers.

And as she combed the tangles from her hair, she found herself wishing she could comb the tangles from her life as easily.

Closing the door to Beatrice's room halfway, Clint found Kristen hovering at his elbow.

"Is she asleep?" Kristen peeked past him into the darkened room, the warmth of her whisper brushing his jaw.

"Yeah." For the past forty-five minutes, while he and Beatrice ate and he tucked her in—at the little girl's request—Kristen had kept a low profile. He wanted to know why. Turning toward her, he gestured toward the living room. "Shall we? I saved you some pizza."

"Thanks, but I'm not hungry. Did Beatrice eat much?"

"Three hearty pieces. Not bad for a nine-year-old girl."

"Thank goodness." Relief smoothed some of the tautness from her features as she walked toward the living room. "I haven't been able to get her to eat more than a few mouthfuls at any one sitting since Sunday. She's going to waste away without more nourishment—and she's tiny to begin with."

He gave her a discerning glance as he followed. "You look like you've lost a few pounds in the past week, too. When's the last time *you* had a decent meal?"

The sudden creases in her brow gave him his answer even before she spoke. "I don't know."

"Eat some pizza." Without waiting for her to consent, he crossed to the kitchen, pulled open the oven door and drew out a plate with several pieces on it. He set it on the dinette table, added a few napkins and opened the cupboard. "What do you want to drink?"

"Soda."

"Sit." He indicated the table.

He wasn't surprised when she acquiesced without argument. From the slump of her shoulders, it was clear her usual spunk had deserted her.

As she slid into a chair and picked up a piece of pizza, he flipped on the coffee-maker. He had a feeling he was going to need the bracing boost of caffeine once they got into her story—the next item on his agenda.

He fiddled around in the kitchen, leaving her in peace while she finished off two slices, but as she began to nibble halfheartedly on the third he joined her.

"Thanks for doing this." She gestured to the pizza and toward Beatrice's bedroom. "I was at my wit's end."

"You want to tell me what's going on?"

She picked at the edge of the crust, scraping off the burnt pieces with her fingernail, leaving the tender dough below exposed. "It's a long story."

"I have all evening."

When she remained silent, he resorted to questions. "Are you related to Beatrice?"

"Yes." She moistened her lips and swallowed, but offered nothing more.

Okay. He'd come back to that. "How long will she be here?"

She crumpled her paper napkin into a tight ball in her fist and gave him a direct look. "Forever. I'm her…her mother."

He stared at her, trying to reconcile that bombshell with what he already knew. "I thought you said her parents were killed in a plane crash?"

"Her adoptive parents were. I'm her birth mother. I had her at the end of my senior year in college and gave her up for adoption. I haven't seen her since the day she was born."

While her gaze didn't waver during that

admission, fear bloomed in her eyes and she started to tremble.

The reason was obvious.

She thought he was going to judge her. Reject her.

And God forgive him, he was tempted to do both. Having a baby out of wedlock went against everything he believed.

On the other hand, who was he to point fingers, a man who'd made plenty of mistakes himself?

At least her mistakes hadn't killed anyone.

Wrapping his fingers around the mug, he forced himself to take a slow, steadying breath. "Do you want to tell me about it?"

"Do you want to hear it?"

No, he didn't. What he wanted was for life to be simple, uncomplicated and rosy.

But maybe that only happened in the kind of storybook he'd read to Beatrice tonight.

As the silence lengthened, he saw a flicker of anguish in Kristen's eyes.

You're blowing it, Nolan.

She started to rise, and he reached out and took her arm. "Yes. I want to hear it."

For a few seconds, as she searched his face, her posture remained taut.

He didn't blink. Didn't look away. Didn't let one iota of censure creep into his eyes.

In the end, to his relief, she sank back into her seat.

"I'm going to have to tell my story—or parts of it—to everyone here anyway. I might as well start with you." She rested an elbow on the table and massaged her temples. "I'll give you the condensed version. I met Beatrice's father in the middle of my junior year of college. He was the big-man-on-campus type, with a lot of big-city glitz, an abundance of confidence and more family money than he knew what to do with. I was surprised he even noticed me—and impressed that he respected my old-fashioned principles about intimacy."

She took a drink of her soda, then placed the glass precisely back in the ring of condensation on the table. "Once I met him, he became the center of my life. My other campus friends fell by the wayside. I was totally smitten. Young love and all that." She tried for a smile, but the twist of her lips reflected more pain than pleasure.

Clint sipped his coffee, giving her the space and time she needed to get her story out.

After a few beats of silence, she picked up the tale.

"Everything was fine until we went to a frat party in September of my senior year. He'd had an internship on the East Coast over the summer, and I'd been working in Wisconsin, trying to help my mom pay down my dad's medical bills. Anyway, we celebrated our reunion with too much liquor. Throw in a few too many pent-up hormones, plus the crushing grief over my dad's death that sent me looking for escape in all the wrong places, and things got out of hand. The rest is history."

It wasn't the first such story Clint had heard. Excess alcohol was notorious for eroding moral standards. It had happened to one of his own buddies in college, a guy whose ethical code Clint had always respected. Except that guy had done the decent thing and offered to marry the girl.

"What did the father say about all this?"

She gave a soft, mirthless laugh. "His exact words were 'What are you going to do about it?'"

"What a…" He bit back the word on the tip of his tongue and cleared his throat.

"Yeah. My sentiments exactly. So much for true love."

"How did your family react?"

She traced the trail of liquid left by a bead of condensation on the side of the glass. "I never told them. Or anyone else, except him and the woman I worked with at the adoption agency. I was too ashamed."

He frowned, trying to get his arms around that. "How did you manage to keep it a secret? It's not easy to hide a pregnancy."

"Easier than you think. The only time that year I went home was for Christmas, and I was just four months along. I was hardly showing. Once my boyfriend dumped me, I stayed in my room when I wasn't in class. No one on campus noticed...or cared...what was happening with my life. I never did get that big, and bulky sweatshirts cover a multitude of sins—literally, in my case. I had the baby before my family came for graduation. It was like it never happened." She swallowed. Sniffed. "So now you know the whole sordid story."

As she waited for him to respond, Clint gripped his mug. Whatever he said next could seal the fate of their relationship.

Lord, give me the strength to leave judgment in Your hands. Grace me with tolerance and understanding. Send me the words that will help erase the hurt from Kristen's heart and heal her soul.

"I'm not certain a mistake of any kind can be classified as sordid." He spoke slowly, choosing his words with care. "You may have used poor judgment by drinking too much, but the choices you made while you were in that impaired condition were compromised. The conscious, cold-sober choice your boyfriend made to leave you in the lurch, however—that's sordid." He tamped down the sudden flare of anger that licked at his gut. He'd never believed in physical violence, but if that jerk was standing here now he'd be tempted to punch him out.

She bit her lower lip as she regarded him. "The fact I had a baby out of wedlock doesn't bother you?"

"Yeah. It does." He folded his hands on the table. He wasn't going to lie. "But I admire the choice you made once you realized you were pregnant."

Her expression grew skeptical. "You think I was right to give away my child?"

"I was talking about the fact you didn't take the easy way out."

She sent him a puzzled look. "But I did take the easy way out."

"I meant abortion."

The shock and revulsion on her face told him more about the character of the woman across from him than did her words. "That wasn't even an option."

"That's what I mean. You took the high road."

"No, I didn't." She leaned toward him intently, her features taut. "What kind of woman gives away her child for adoption if she has the means and resources to take care of it? And I did. My mother would have helped me, but I couldn't face the shame. I didn't want to disappoint my family. I didn't want to admit I'd made a mistake, that their golden girl wasn't perfect." She rested her elbows on the table and dropped her head in her hands. "It was a selfish choice. All I cared about was me, and protecting my pride."

He knew all about pride—and its tragic repercussions.

But they weren't talking about his issues tonight.

He shifted gears, taking a moment to sift through all he knew about this woman. And slowly the pieces began to fall into place. She'd told him once she didn't make friends or put down roots. Now he knew why.

She didn't think she deserved a husband or family.

That was the price she'd paid for her mistake. Sentencing herself to a solitary life was her way of seeking atonement.

"Kristen." He touched her hand, waiting until she lifted her head. "We all make mistakes—and God is willing to forgive those who repent."

Her eyes were haunted as she locked gazes with him. "I gave away my daughter, Clint, and I didn't have to. I don't deserve forgiveness."

"He thinks you do. That's why He sent His son to die for our sins. Have you ever asked for forgiveness?"

"No. I was too ashamed. A child is a gift, no matter the circumstances of conception, and I threw it away."

"That's a pretty harsh indictment. Are you telling me you didn't go to a reputable adoption agency?"

"No. The campus chaplain put me in touch with the one I used. They were very professional."

"Do you think they chose inappropriate adoptive parents?"

"No. I was involved in the process. I read all their background material and helped pick them. They seemed like wonderful people."

"Did they treat Beatrice well?"

"Very."

"How do you know?"

"It's obvious she loved them, and she always looked happy in the photos I received through the agency twice a year. That was one of my requirements for the adoption. I might have given her up, but I couldn't bear the thought of losing touch completely."

That explained the album he'd seen on the coffee table.

"So you went through a minister to find an adoption agency, participated in the selection of the couple and followed your daughter's progress through the years. That doesn't sound unredeemably selfish to me."

Her shoulders hunched. "You're putting a better spin on this than I deserve."

"I don't think so. You were young and desperate and your serious boyfriend deserted you to deal with the crisis alone as you were also trying to deal with grief over your father's death. I think you made remarkably good choices in light of all that. And now you've been given a second chance. How did that come about, anyway?"

He listened as she recounted the call from the woman at the adoption agency and her conversation with the attorney who'd shared the wishes Beatrice's adoptive parents had outlined in their will.

"To be honest, when Connie called I had a lot of the same feelings I had the first time around." Kristen laced her fingers so tight the blood drained from the knuckles. "Shame and fear and panic and desperation. And once again, my pride got in the way."

"Yet in the end, you overcame it and followed your heart. That's all that counts."

"But Beatrice hates me."

"She doesn't even know you yet."

"She knows I gave her away."

"Give her some time to adjust. She's got a lot of stuff to deal with all at once. It has to be overwhelming for a little kid."

"It's overwhelming for a big kid, too. I'm not sure I'm equipped to deal with a childhood trauma of this magnitude." She rose, her agitation evident in every jerky movement as she began to pace. "But the only other option was foster care. I have to believe that would have been worse."

He stood more slowly. Kristen needed comforting as much as Beatrice did—but would she accept it from him?

Trusting his instincts, he caught her hand as she passed, linking her trembling fingers with his. "I have every confidence you're equipped to give Beatrice all the love and care and compassion she needs. A woman who makes cookies for neighbors and takes in stray kittens must have a kind and tender heart."

A slight flush restored some of the

color to her cheeks. "About the kitten…I don't let Clyde in, in case you're worried. I know you have a no-pets policy, and I wouldn't…"

"Kristen." He stepped closer and took her upper arms in a firm but gentle grasp. "I'm not worried about the provisions of your lease. I'm worried about you."

She scrutinized his face. "Why?"

"I like you. And even though you're not in the market for a relationship, I want you to know I'm here if you need a helping hand with anything."

Tears welled in her eyes. "I appreciate that, but I think everything's under control—except my relationship with Beatrice. I did arrange to have her bedroom furniture shipped here, though, so I can re-create a familiar environment for her. Maybe that will help."

"Any pressure at work because of the emergency time off?"

"No. Louis Mattson has been more than understanding, probably because I've never taken more than half my vacation. And the assistant concierges are up to speed. Day care's the big issue."

"There's a woman in town who's watched children for other people on occasion. The stepson of the foreman on the inn construction project was one of her charges for a while. I can give you her name, if you like."

"That would be great."

"Are you certain there's nothing else you need?"

Instead of responding in words, she closed her eyes and swayed toward him a fraction—as if she wanted to be held.

Without stopping to consider whether his actions were wise, he closed the space between them and pulled her into a hug. She stiffened, but he didn't let her go.

"Relax." Cheek against her hair, her unique fragrance enveloping him, he had to remind himself his gesture was meant to comfort, nothing more. "It's just a hug. Hold on and breathe."

For an instant she remained rigid. Then slowly, very slowly, she relaxed. Her arms crept around him, and she did hold on. Tight.

"Better?" He murmured the question against her temple.

"Yeah." The word came out in a ragged whoosh of air. "But it's also dangerous. I could get used to this."

"Maybe that's okay."

Even as he said the words, he regretted them. Kristen had been through enough trauma in her life; he shouldn't be suggesting a scenario he himself wasn't yet certain was wise.

A few beats of silence passed, and then she eased away from him, regret pooling in those jade irises. "No, it's not. Hugs can lead to more serious things, and I need to sort out all the other complications in my life before I even think about whether there's a place in it for romance."

This time he remained silent.

When he didn't reply, she tucked her hair behind her ear and edged toward the door. "It's been a long day. I'm about ready to fold. Thank you again for all your help—and for the pizza."

"No problem." He followed her to the door. "I'll call you with a number for Ruth Watson, the babysitter I mentioned. She's a great gal with a bunch of kids. I think you'll like her. When are you going back to work?"

"Monday." She twisted the knob and pulled the door open.

With no further reason to linger, he exited with a quiet *good night* and started down the steps.

At the bottom, he paused to take a few deep breaths of the clear, clean air and to send a silent request heavenward for the troubled duo occupying his second floor.

Just as the motion-sensitive light he'd activated above Kristen's door went out, he heard the door open again. Staying in the shadows, he repositioned himself to get a view of the landing. Kristen exited, carton of milk in hand, and bent to fill the small, shallow bowl.

She was taking care of the stray kitten—just as she wanted to take care of the daughter who'd lost the only family she'd ever known.

Melting Beatrice's heart wasn't going to be as easy as winning the loyalty of a kitten. That would take a lot more than a bowl of two-percent milk. But the milk of human kindness should eventually convince the little girl that Kristen did, indeed, love her.

Until then, however, he suspected his tenant was in for a rocky ride.

Chapter Ten

Kristen smiled at the honeymooning couple across from her at the concierge desk. "Of course, breakfast here at the inn by the pool is always wonderful. But since you'd like to sample some local fare, I recommend the Orchid Café in town. The home cooking is terrific, and the cinnamon rolls are to die for."

The phone on her desk in the lobby began to ring, and she cast a discreet glance at the ID. Mark Stephens's number. She'd checked in with him as soon as she'd arrived two hours ago, to catch up on the opening week she'd missed. Why would he be calling her this soon?

"That sounds like fun, honey. Let's give it a try." The bride reached for her new husband's hand.

"Your wish is my command." He gave her a mock bow, then turned back to Kristen. "Thanks for the recommendation. They're open on Monday, right?"

"Every day but Sunday. Let me know how you enjoy it."

As they walked away, she grabbed the phone before it could roll to voice mail. "Hi, Mark."

"Are you with a guest?"

"Just finished."

"I've been on the phone with Mr. Mattson. He'd like you to call him ASAP about Starfish Bay's Labor Day celebration."

"What about it?"

"One of the sisters from the Orchid mentioned it to him at the open house. He thinks we should participate in some way, and he wants you to spearhead the effort."

Kristen closed her eyes. As if she didn't have enough on her plate the first day back on the job—not to mention a daughter who cried herself to sleep each night but rebuffed any consolation attempts, who continued to eat like a bird and who spoke only if spoken to...except yesterday, when she'd asked why they weren't going to church.

Could things get any more complicated?

"Kristen? You there?"

"Yes. I'll give him a call as soon as we hang up."

"Look...I know you're dealing with a bunch of personal stuff right now. We can pull other people in on this if we need to."

"I appreciate that, Mark." She bit her bottom lip, fighting back the temptation to take advantage of the man's offer. But she'd always carried her weight at work, and she didn't want to slack off now—especially when she might need other favors down the road. "I'll let you know if I need help. For now, though, everything's under control. I can handle the festival project."

"Okay. If the situation changes, let me know."

The man severed the connection, and

after giving herself a minute to psych herself up for the call, Kristen tapped in Louis Mattson's number. His secretary put her through at once.

"Hello, Kristen. Everything okay on the home front? Your daughter settling in?"

"Thank you for asking. So far, so good." Hardly. But the president of Mattson Properties didn't need to hear the details of her depressing tale. She was just grateful he'd accepted her thirty-second, top-line explanation at face value after Connie called, and then told her to take as much time as she needed despite the opening. *Thank You, God, for a considerate boss.* "I understand you'd like us to participate in the town's Labor Day festivities."

"Yes. The sisters at the Orchid told me it's a town tradition, and I'd like the inn to have a sponsorship presence. I believe the festival will be discussed in detail at the town council meeting tomorrow night."

"Then I'll be there."

"Perfect. Plan on a budget similar to the one you had for the Starfish Bay open house, but if you need more, let me know. I want to maintain a friendly, cooperative relationship with the town."

"That amount should be more than enough to give a nice boost to their celebration."

"Excellent. Let me know how things progress. And good luck on the home front."

As Kristen thanked him and put the handset back in its cradle, she studied the sea through the expansive wall of windows on the Pacific side of the inn. The sun was glistening on the water, a few lazy white clouds drifted across the deep blue sky and a ship on the distant horizon was moving steadily toward its destination.

The panorama was placid and calming—exactly the kind of get-away-from-it-all experience Mattson Properties' guests were after. Most returned home refreshed, relaxed and reinvigorated.

But even the soothing ambience of an upscale Mattson inn couldn't quell the churning that had started in Kristen's stomach with Connie's call and intensified with each passing day.

So far, her efforts to connect with Beatrice had yielded zero results. Now doubts were beginning to creep in. Maybe she hadn't done the child any favors by taking her in. Perhaps Beatrice would have done better in a foster environment, where there was no baggage—and no birth mother to resent.

Her throat tightened, and she looked away from the serene view as she sent yet another silent prayer heavenward.

Please, Lord, show me how to reach her!

As Clint took his seat next to Lindsey at the head table reserved for town council members, he surveyed the hall. Since the contentious issue over development of The Point had erupted a year and a half ago, attendance at the meetings had picked up. At least fifty people were present on this Tuesday night, even though nothing momentous was on the agenda.

Halfway through his scan of the residents, he found himself staring into a pair of familiar green eyes.

Kristen was here? With Beatrice? What was going on?

As he settled into his seat, he did a quick assessment of his tenant. He'd seen little of her in the past few days, now that his summer schedule had kicked in and he was working more weekends. But she seemed wearier than she had at their last encounter—and more stressed.

The blonde girl beside her gave him a tentative smile, and he smiled back. When Kristen looked down at her daughter, however, the child's smile faded and she scooted to the far edge of her seat, clutching her worn Raggedy Ann doll tighter. A flicker of distress tightened Kristen's features.

Obviously things hadn't improved between the two of them.

"All right...I think we're ready to begin." Mayor Susan Peroni stood, greeted everyone and called the meeting to order.

Clint only half listened to the secretary's

reading of the minutes from the last meeting as he tried to figure out why Kristen was here.

But he got his answer once the mayor introduced the topic of the town's Labor Day festival. Susan ran through the schedule of events, pausing at the end to peruse the crowd over the top of her half-glasses. "Any comments or questions?"

Kristen raised her hand.

"Hello, Kristen. Nice to see you. You, too, Beatrice." Susan smiled at the little girl, who burrowed deeper in her doll. "Did you have a question?"

"No." Kristen stood. "I have an offer. Mr. Mattson would like the inn to be part of the festival, perhaps in some sort of sponsorship capacity. I'd be happy to work with someone on the council to see how we might contribute to the event."

Susan smiled at her. "Now isn't that fine? I knew the inn would be a blessing for this town." She sent an I-told-you-so look toward Lindsey, who rolled her eyes, then turned her attention to him. "Clint, would you like to get together with Kristen to discuss this, since you're taking the lead on this year's festival?"

"I'll be happy to."

"Excellent. We have sponsors for the parade and craft fair, but we're always open to new suggestions. And we can add some events on Sunday if we have a new sponsor, make a whole weekend out of it." She smiled at Kristen again. "We're very grateful for any assistance Mattson Properties is willing to provide."

"I'll talk with you after the meeting." Clint directed his comment to Kristen, who acknowledged it with a dip of her head as she retook her seat.

Susan wrapped things up quickly after that, and as the crowd dispersed, Clint wove through several chatting clusters of townspeople toward Kristen.

"This is a surprise." He smiled at her, then at Beatrice.

"For me, too." She tucked her hair behind her ear and hitched her purse higher on her shoulder. "Mr. Mattson called yesterday.

The sisters mentioned the festival to him at the open house." She inspected the emptying room. "Would you like to talk here or at the house? Or is another time better?"

He checked his watch, formulating a plan as he spoke. "Now is fine. Why don't we go to the Orchid? If we hurry, we should be able to squeeze in before they shut down for the night. And I'd be willing to bet we could rustle up a piece of Lillian's chocolate Oreo pie—if anyone happens to like chocolate."

He glanced down at Beatrice, whose expression brightened.

Bingo.

"I hate to impose on your time."

He transferred his attention back to his tenant and gave a subtle tip of his head toward her daughter. "I don't mind, and I have a hankering for one of the Orchid's desserts myself."

She checked on her daughter, who still wore an interested look, and capitulated. "Okay. We'll meet you there in five minutes."

"Sounds great. I'll gather up my things."

As he rejoined Lindsey at the head table, his fellow council member tucked her notes into a small satchel and gestured toward the departing duo. "Nice woman."

"Very." He busied himself collecting his own papers.

"That was a short meeting, though."

"We're going to continue it at the Orchid." He tapped his notes into a neat pile and slid them into a folder.

"Ah." Lindsey picked up her purse and wiggled her eyebrows. "Have fun."

He frowned. "This isn't a date."

"Isn't it?" She grinned at him.

"We're going to talk about the Labor Day celebration."

"You could do that here."

As he struggled to come up with a response, her grin broadened. "Hey, it's okay. More power to you. But watch out for Lillian and Genevieve. They'll be matching you two up in no time. Take it from one who knows—although I have to say in my case things turned out fine." She leaned past him to smile and wave at the tall man who'd entered the back of the room, lowering her voice. "The sisters had Nate and me pegged from the get-go."

Giving his arm a sympathetic pat, she skirted past him and hurried toward the back of the room to join her husband.

Clint followed more slowly. He knew all about the sisters' propensity for matchmaking. And truth be told, he wasn't averse to some prodding on their part when it came to a certain concierge.

But he had a discouraging feeling said concierge was going to be a hard sell.

"My! Isn't this cozy?" Genevieve beamed at the threesome as she settled them into a booth at the Orchid. "I haven't seen enough of any of you lately. You all must be keeping very busy. But I'm glad you found a few minutes for a social engagement."

Kristen opened her mouth to correct the older woman's assumption, but before she could speak Genevieve addressed Beatrice.

"And how are you liking your new home, young lady?"

Beatrice buried her face in the doll, muffling her response. "Okay."

A flicker of compassion softened Genevieve's eyes. "It's hard to move to a new place, but I have a feeling you'll like it here fine once you get used to it and make some friends."

Her daughter didn't respond.

To Kristen's relief, Clint broke the awkward silence.

"I was telling the ladies about Lillian's chocolate Oreo pie. I think Beatrice might like it."

"I've never met a youngster who didn't." Genevieve smiled at Beatrice. "And I happen to know we have two pieces left. What would you folks like?"

"Coffee for me." Kristen folded her hands on the table.

"Is that all?" Genevieve gave her a disappointed look.

"Why don't we split that second piece of pie?" Clint suggested.

Rather than debate the matter, she nodded. "That's fine."

"I'll have some coffee, too," he told Genevieve. "Beatrice, what would you like to drink?"

"Milk."

"Milk, pie and coffee." Genevieve ticked off their orders. "Got it. I'll be back with everything in a jiffy."

As the café owner took off for the kitchen, Kristen checked on Beatrice, who was seated between her and Clint. Bringing her along to the meeting tonight hadn't been optimal, but her daughter had spent all day with Ruth Watson and her brood. She didn't want to pass her off in the evening, too. Still, it was clear she'd rather be anywhere than here—despite the chocolate-pie bribe.

"So what did you have in mind for the Labor Day festival?"

At Clint's query, she forced herself to change gears. "I'm open to suggestions."

His expression grew thoughtful as Genevieve deposited their drinks and departed for the kitchen again. "It might be nice to plan something for Sunday, as Susan suggested. It doesn't have to be elaborate. Maybe it could be an event geared toward families and children."

"I'm more experienced at planning things for couples." Kristen stirred some cream into her coffee. "I don't know what children would enjoy."

"We have an expert on that demographic right here." Clint smiled down at her daughter. "Let's start with food. What's your favorite thing to eat, Beatrice?"

The girl scrunched up her face and chewed at her lower lip as she considered the question. "Ice cream."

Kristen filed away that new piece of information. Her own queries along those lines had been met with disinterested shrugs.

"Ice cream." Clint set his elbow on the table and gave Beatrice his full attention. "I like that. The inn could sponsor an ice-cream social at the nature preserve on The Point. It would be a perfect opportunity to introduce the residents who haven't made it down there yet to the interpretive trail, too. What do you think?"

Her daughter gave a solemn nod. "That would be nice. But I think you should have cupcakes, too. And lemonade."

"Excellent idea. What do you think, Kristen?"

"Sounds perfect to me."

"More than perfect. I understand Starfish Bay Chapel used to sponsor a popular ice-cream social, so we'd be reviving a much-loved tradition. Lindsey at the Mercantile remembers it." Clint took a sip of his coffee.

"Remembers what?" Genevieve bustled over and set their pie on the table, along with an extra fork for Kristen.

"The annual ice-cream social."

"Oh, I remember that, too! A lovely event. It was held every year until poor Reverend Tobias died and the chapel was closed."

"The inn is thinking about bringing it

back for the Labor Day festival. It was Beatrice's idea."

"And a fine idea it is, too." Genevieve patted the girl's shoulder, and Beatrice gave her a shy smile.

"We're working out the details now."

"Well, don't let me interrupt. Wait till I tell Lillian!" She hurried back toward the kitchen.

Clint picked up the extra fork and handed it to Kristen, gesturing toward the pie. "I'll warn you in advance—it's addictive."

"This is really good." Beatrice hadn't waited for an invitation to dig into her dessert. She was eating with more gusto than she'd exhibited since arriving in Starfish Bay—thanks to the man who was sharing their booth. Once again, her landlord had managed to engage her daughter.

Latching onto his approach, she broke off a modest bite of the pie. "What else do you think we should have at this ice-cream social, Beatrice?" She forked the creamy confection into her mouth, praying her daughter wouldn't shut down.

The child poked at her dessert while Kristen held her breath. "A face painter would be fun."

Kristen exhaled. "I like that idea."

"And a magician. I saw one once at a friend's birthday party. Or someone who makes animals and stuff out of balloons."

"Those are all great suggestions." Kristen took another bite of the pie Clint pushed back her direction after his own sample. "What kind of cupcakes should we get?"

"Chocolate." Her daughter demolished the last bite of her dessert. "But I guess you should get some vanilla ones, too, in case someone doesn't like chocolate."

"And what flavors of ice cream?"

"Chocolate."

Over her daughter's head, Clint smiled. "I'm picking up a pattern here."

"And chocolate chip," Beatrice added.

"I better make a list." Kristen dug around in her purse for a piece of paper, and Clint handed over his pen in silence as he sipped his coffee.

With her daughter watching as she wrote,

she listed all the items they'd discussed. "Anything else?"

"I'll think about it." Beatrice settled back in her seat.

Tucking the paper back in her purse, she handed Clint his pen back and tried to think of another topic that would keep her daughter engaged. Nothing came to mind.

As if sensing her dilemma, Clint stepped back in. "So what do you think of Clyde, Beatrice?"

Her face went blank. "Who's Clyde?"

Clint's questioning gaze flicked to Kristen. "She hasn't met Clyde?"

"I usually feed him after Beatrice goes to bed." Kristen speared the final bite of pie. "I didn't want attachments to form, given the house rules and all."

"Who's Clyde?" Beatrice looked from one to the other as she repeated her question.

"A kitten your…Kristen…adopted." Clint set his mug back on the table.

"You have a kitten?" Beatrice stared at her.

"He's not mine. He just started showing up, so I give him a bowl of milk every night. But I never bring him inside." She directed the last statement to Clint.

"Are you going to feed him tonight?"

"Yes."

"Can I help?"

"Animals do seem to bring people together." Clint was still watching her.

So far, he'd been batting a thousand with her daughter—and she didn't intend to break that streak.

"Sure. I've been leaving the milk on the landing, but maybe tonight we can wait for him to come and all get acquainted. Would you like that?"

Several seconds ticked by. Finally, the little girl nodded. "Yes."

The knot of tension in Kristen's stomach relaxed a hair.

"Speaking of animals…remember the first night you were here, and I told you about my park?" Clint smiled down at Beatrice. "As it turns out, I'm doing a junior ranger program this Saturday at ten. We're going to take a hike and look for banana slugs and explore some of those giant hollowed-out trees. If you two want to come, I'll save you a place."

"Can we?" Beatrice sent her a hopeful look.

Why not? She was off Saturday, and Beatrice seemed to open up a lot more when Clint was around.

"Sounds like a great way to spend a Saturday morning."

For the first time in their acquaintance, her daughter gave her a genuine smile.

And as they finished up their desserts and paid the bill, Kristen allowed herself to hope that maybe…just maybe…things were beginning to look up.

Chapter Eleven

"Maybe he's not going to come." Beatrice rose from the step she'd been sharing with Kristen to scan the wooded terrain around Clint's house. She'd been up and down as much as a seesaw.

Kristen checked her watch. "I'm sure he'll be here, honey. This is earlier than I usually feed him, so we might have to be patient." Clyde hadn't missed a night yet, and she prayed this wouldn't be the first.

The wind picked up, molding Beatrice's jacket to her thin frame, and Kristen yearned to pull her into a protective embrace. But even though they were sharing a step, Beatrice had stayed at the far end.

Now her back was turned as she watched for the kitty—a posture that summed up their relationship.

Kristen sighed. How was she ever going to break through the barriers Beatrice had erected between them? Or, more accurately, the ones she'd erected nine years ago when she'd given her daughter away? The hope that had fanned to life earlier at the Orchid flickered. Her daughter seemed as distant as ever.

All at once, Beatrice's shoulders slumped. "Maybe Clyde died."

At her daughter's soft words, pressure built behind Kristen's eyes. "He's not dead, honey."

"How do you know?" Her words grew shaky and she played with the hem of her jacket. "Sometimes when people don't come back, it's because they died."

Knowing Beatrice might rebuff the overture, Kristen followed her heart anyway and took the young girl's cold fingers in a warm clasp.

Her daughter stiffened, but she didn't pull back.

"He might be scared. He's not used to people waiting for him. Why don't you sit again?" She gave the small fingers in her grasp a gentle tug.

For an instant, Beatrice resisted. Then she sank back onto the step, keeping her distance. But she didn't pull her hand away.

"I always wanted a cat."

Her daughter's quiet admission tightened Kristen's throat. "Why didn't you get one?"

"Mom was allergic to the dander. Dad said we might be able to get a dog, though. He was checking into it when…before they died." Her voice hiccuped and she bowed her head.

Kristen wanted to scoot closer, but holding hands might be a big enough step for one day. "I had lots of pets while I was growing up."

Lifting her chin, Beatrice inched toward her a fraction. "What kind?"

"Dogs. Cats. Horses."

"Horses?" The girl's eyes widened. "Where did you grow up?"

"My mom and dad owned a place in Wisconsin where families used to take vacations. It was kind of like a farm, but nicer than that. It was called Lake Pleasant Inn."

"So it was a hotel? Like the inn where you work now?"

Kristen smiled. "Nothing like that. It wasn't fancy at all. But we loved it anyway."

"Do your mom and dad still have it?"

"No." Kristen swallowed past a wave of melancholy. "My dad died when I was in college. It cost a lot of money to pay for all his doctors' bills, so my mom had to sell the inn. She lives in town now, near my brother." Kristen stroked her thumb along the back of Beatrice's hand, which had warmed. "They're both looking forward to meeting you."

In the deepening dusk, Kristen couldn't make out Beatrice's features—but she had no problem interpreting the retraction of her daughter's hand.

Don't take it personally, Kristen. And don't push. Give her time to adjust. You're making progress. Really.

In the silence that fell between them, Kristen heard a faint meow. Beatrice straightened up and squinted into the shadows at the base of the stairs.

Clyde had timed his entrance perfectly.

"I think our dinner guest has arrived." Kristen whispered the comment as she set the bowl two steps down and picked up the carton of milk.

A few seconds later, a golden ball of fur emerged out of the shadows and began to ascend the stairs.

"Here he comes!"

Beatrice's soft but urgent voice carried down the steps and the kitty paused to inspect them, eyes glowing in the dim light.

Slowly Kristen opened the container of milk and poured it into the bowl. "Here, kitty, kitty. Come have your dinner, Clyde. You have a new friend who wants to meet you."

The cat hesitated.

"He's not going to come." Beatrice's whispered words were laced with disappointment.

"Give him a minute to check us out. Stay very quiet."

She could feel the quivers of excitement running through her daughter, but the little girl did her best not to move.

At last, step by cautious step, the kitty ascended until he was two risers below the bowl of milk.

"Come on, boy. We're your friends." Kristen used a coaxing tone as she bent down, dipped her fingers in the milk and held them out to the cat.

Pausing after every step, he crept forward. After giving her fingers a sniff, he licked at them as she drew them back, close to the bowl of milk at their feet. Once there, he began to drink greedily.

"He looks hungry." Another whisper from Beatrice. "Do you think I can pet him?"

"Let's give him a chance to have dinner first."

They waited while the cat lapped up the milk. As he was finishing, Kristen spoke again. "Hold out your hand to him and let him sniff it. Be very slow and gentle. You don't want to scare him."

Beatrice did as instructed. Clyde stopped drinking to study the small hand a few inches from his nose. He leaned forward. Hesitated. Then he brushed his whiskers against Beatrice's palm and licked it.

Her daughter's sudden giggle surprised Kristen as much as it did the cat.

It was the most beautiful sound she'd ever heard.

"His tongue is tickling me."

"I bet it is. Go ahead and talk to him, honey."

"Hi, Clyde. My name's Beatrice." She leaned closer to the cat. "I've heard all about how you come here to eat every night. Would it be okay if I pet you?"

Kristen was about to tell Beatrice cats didn't understand human language when Clyde nosed up the steps, past the empty bowl, climbed into the little girl's lap and gave an expectant purr.

How about that?

Propping her back against the wall of the house, Kristen watched the two of them interact. The cat batted at Beatrice's fingers as she played with him, producing more giggles from her daughter. Based on his contented meows, Clyde was enjoying the interaction, too.

But finally, with a languid stretch, he leaped to the steps. After one more look in Beatrice's direction and a final meow, he bounded down the stairs and disappeared into the shadows.

Beatrice rose and stared after him. "Do you think he'll come back tomorrow?"

"No question about it." Kristen picked up the empty bowl and container of milk and stood, too. "He knows where the food is. And now he has a friend, too." She started up the stairs to the landing, Beatrice following.

"Rose says I can be her friend, too."

Rose. Kristen tried to place the name as she ushered Beatrice through the door.

"You know. Rose Watson. Her mom watches me during the day."

"Oh, right." The red-haired girl with pigtails who was always hanging out the car window when Ruth stopped by the inn to pick up Beatrice in the morning.

"And Clint is our friend, too, isn't he?"

"Yes." At the very least.

Kristen slid the carton of milk back in the fridge and moved to the sink to rinse the milk bowl. To her surprise, Beatrice stayed on her heels, still talking, still engaged.

"I didn't think when I came here I'd ever be happy again. But I was happy tonight at the Orchid. And sometimes I laugh with Rose. I felt happy while I was holding Clyde a few minutes ago, too." She played with the zipper on her jacket, her expression troubled. "Is that wrong?"

Wrong? Kristen struggled with that question as she dried her hands—until understanding suddenly dawned. Beatrice felt guilty for the fleeting moments of joy she'd experienced in the past few weeks because she believed she should be grieving over the parents she'd lost.

It was the same dichotomy Kristen herself had struggled with after she'd given up her daughter for adoption. For years she'd felt guilty about any moments of happiness that came her way.

Sometimes she still did.

Dropping down to one knee, she took her daughter's hands. They'd grown cold again.

"No, honey. It's not wrong. Losing people we love is very sad. But God doesn't want us to be sad forever, and neither would the people we love. Don't you think your mom and dad would want you to be happy again?"

She bit her lower lip. "I guess. But I'm afraid if I stop thinking about them all the time, I'll forget them."

Tears pricked Kristen's eyes. "You won't. Because they'll always be in your heart. And after a while, you'll remember all the happy things you did with them instead of being sad. That's how it was with my dad."

Beatrice dipped her chin and scuffed the toe of her shoe. "I've been wondering why my mom and dad...why they let you take me back."

Inhaling a deep, calming breath, Kristen framed her response with care. "I think it was because they knew it was hard for me to let you go in the first place. And I made them promise to send me pictures of you every year, so they knew I wanted to be part of your life."

Beatrice tipped up her chin. "You have pictures of me?"

Rising, Kristen took her hand. "A lot of them. I'll show you."

She led the little girl down the hall to her own room, motioned to her bed and pulled the album out of the closet as Beatrice scooted onto the mattress. Sitting beside her, she opened the book and they paged through it together.

Beatrice didn't say much, except to identify a few of the occasions in the photos.

But at the end, after Kristen closed the album, her daughter looked up at her.

"Do you love me?"

Tears blurred Kristen's vision as she choked out her response. "With all my heart."

Several beats of silence ticked by. Kristen didn't expect a reciprocal sentiment. She was more than happy to settle for the quick touch of Beatrice's hand on her cheek before her daughter slipped off the bed with a quiet *good night* and disappeared down the hall toward her room.

Placing her palm flat on the spot Beatrice had touched, Kristen closed her eyes. They had a long road to travel to establish the kind of relationship she longed to have with her daughter.

But tonight had been a promising first step.

"Redwoods might be giants, but they all start small, either from tiny seeds like this—" Clint held out his palm and the eight junior rangers gathered around

"—or from sprouts off of the stump of an old tree, like that one." He gestured to a downed giant behind him. "And the ones that begin as sprouts usually grow in a circle, around the stump. How many sprouts do you think can grow from one tree that falls down?"

"Twenty?" That guess was offered by a towheaded boy of about nine.

"Why don't we find out? Let's count them together."

From her spot on the sidelines with some of the other parents, Kristen watched as Clint led his junior rangers around a circle of sprouts, counting aloud with them as the group made the circuit.

The man knew his stuff. And he knew how to share it with kids in a manner that fanned their interest and enthusiasm. So far, his junior rangers had gotten down on their hands and knees to observe a banana slug's habitat up close; learned about the redwoods' resistance to fire by going inside the hollowed-out base of a living tree to examine the thick bark; and felt droplets of water that had condensed on the crowns and dripped down to the roots, thanks to the fog the trees themselves had created as part of their built-in watering system.

Kristen had been as enthralled as the kids.

And Beatrice was eating it up.

Smiling, Kristen watched her daughter's animated face as she counted along with the rest of the group while Clint led them like the Pied Piper around the circle of the sprouting stump.

As he wrapped up the hour-long session and escorted his young students and their parents back to the visitor center, he pointed out other items of interest along the way. But Kristen found herself focusing more on the man's broad shoulders than the natural wonders around her.

And wishing she'd met someone like him a long time ago—before life had grown complicated.

To his credit, he hadn't seemed put off by her past. He'd also connected well with Beatrice—far better than she had. Still…why would someone like him, who appeared to have his act totally together, be interested in a woman with so much baggage?

"That's it for today." Clint stopped and smiled down at the children clustered around him. "What was your favorite part of the hike?"

A chorus of answers rang out, and Clint spoke with each child before sending them off to their parents. He finished with Beatrice.

"Well, what did you think of my land of the giants?" He dropped down to balance on the balls of his feet beside her as Kristen approached.

"It was awesome."

Clint transferred his gaze to her, and one side of his mouth quirked up. "I think someone had fun."

"Can we come again?" Beatrice addressed that query to her.

"Of course." Kristen stopped beside them. "I couldn't hear your answer when Clint asked what your favorite part was."

"I liked the hollow tree that was as big as my old room at home."

Home. As in Denver.

Kristen tried not to let that bother her.

"But I think I liked the sunbeams coming through the trees best. It reminded me of God. The sun used to come through the windows of our church just like that. It always made me feel like God was close by. I felt like that here, too."

Clint squeezed her shoulder. "That's exactly how I feel in the forest, especially when the rays of the sun filter through the trees. It's like light from heaven."

"I miss going to church." Beatrice swiveled toward her, and Kristen braced herself for the question she knew was coming. "Can we go tomorrow?"

She could feel Clint's scrutiny as he stood.

"Like I told you last week, Beatrice, I'm pretty new here, too. I haven't had a chance to check out the churches."

Her daughter eyed Clint. "Do you go to church?"

He hesitated, sending Kristen an apologetic look as he responded. "Yes."

"We could go to his church."

How was she supposed to get out of this?

"Um…I'll have to think about it, honey."

Beatrice made a face and lifted her chin. "That's what you said last week. Are you mad at God or something?"

"No." Her denial was swift—and sure. She'd never been mad at God. But He had a right to be mad at her.

Her daughter's skeptical expression told Kristen the little girl wasn't buying her reply. "You told me I shouldn't be mad at Him, even though He let my mom and dad die."

"I'm not mad at Him, Beatrice."

"Then why won't you go?"

She tried—and failed—to think of a plausible reason.

Okay. Time to regroup. If it gave Beatrice some measure of comfort, made her feel more at home, what could be the harm in attending a Sunday service on occasion?

"I guess we can go, if Clint will give us directions."

"I can do better than that." He'd taken a discreet step back during their exchange, but now he rejoined the conversation. "Why don't you ride with me? The church is in Trinidad, which isn't far, but there's no sense taking two vehicles."

"Are you certain? I don't want to impose."

The slow smile he gave her sent a tingle up Kristen's spine.

"I'm certain. It's been a long while since I escorted two lovely ladies to church."

That elicited a giggle from Beatrice. "I'm not a lady. I'm a little girl."

"You'll be a lady someday." He smiled and touched the tip of her nose before turning his attention to Kristen. "There's a ten o'clock service. I try to leave by nine-thirty."

"We'll be ready. And now we need to let you get back to work." The rest of his junior rangers and their parents had wandered off while they talked.

"Duty does call. But I'll look forward to seeing you both tomorrow." With a parting touch to the wide brim of his hat, he took off toward the visitor center.

Beatrice watched him for a few seconds. "I like him. He's nice."

"Yes, he is." Too nice for her. That was the problem. He deserved a woman as together as he seemed to be.

Kristen started toward the parking lot, Beatrice beside her.

"He reminds me of my dad. Not in looks, though. My dad's hair had a lot of gray in it, and he wasn't as tall, but he always listened to me, like Clint does. A lot of grown-ups don't listen to kids."

"I'd be happy to listen if you ever want to talk."

"But you're gone a lot."

For the first time, Kristen fully understood the conflict—and guilt—working mothers faced. That remark was like a direct hit in the solar plexus.

She paused at the car and dropped down on one knee beside Beatrice. "I have to work, honey. That's how I make the money to pay our bills."

"My mom didn't work."

"She was very lucky to be able to stay at home with you. That can happen if a little boy or girl has a mom *and* a dad."

"Maybe someday you'll get married."

An image of the tall ranger flashed across her mind, but she quickly squelched it. Despite the sentiment on the place mats at the Orchid, she wasn't going to start believing that wishes—or dreams—could come true. Even in Starfish Bay.

Standing, she reached for the car door. "I suppose that could happen. In the meantime, we need to take a look through your clothes and find a pretty outfit for you to wear to church tomorrow."

Beatrice climbed into the car and buckled her seat belt. "Are you going to wear something pretty, too?"

"Yes."

"God will like that."

"I'm sure He will."

But as she shut the door and circled

around to the driver's side, Kristen was more interested in a certain ranger's reaction to her attire.

Heaven forgive her.

Willing to all driver police tonight was
the moneylend end a Christmas of wear
not to be think.
Heaven from to her

Chapter Twelve

As the organist played the closing hymn, Clint slanted a sidelong glance over Beatrice's head at the slender woman whose attention was focused on the sanctuary.

He should be singing. Or praying. Or meditating. But in that delicate silky dress that swirled around her knees and softly molded her curves, Kristen was one big distraction. His concentration had been off for the whole service.

Truth be told, he was still finding it hard to believe she'd come. Until the moment she'd climbed into his truck, he'd expected her to find some excuse to back out. If it hadn't been for her daughter's persistence, she probably would have. She'd been honest about her estrangement from God, and despite their discussion on the subject, he didn't think he'd persuaded her she was worthy of forgiveness or second chances.

Yet based on her peaceful expression, he had a feeling she wasn't sorry she'd come.

And that was good. Because he'd been honest with her, too. If he ever got serious about a woman, she'd have to share his faith. Relationships faced enough unforeseen obstacles; adding more by choice was foolish.

As if sensing his perusal, Kristen turned her head toward him. He had a tiny window of opportunity to look away and pretend he hadn't been staring…but chose not to. Instead, he gave her a slow smile—and watched soft color steal over her cheeks.

"Are we leaving now?"

At Beatrice's question and the tug on his sleeve, he pulled his gaze away from Kristen to respond to the little girl. "What?"

"Isn't it time to leave?"

He checked out the church. The organ

had gone quiet, and the pews were emptying. "Yeah, it is."

Exiting into the aisle, he ushered them out. As Kristen passed, a faint whiff of the fragrance that was all her drifted his way, and he leaned closer to inhale it.

Mmm.

He could get used to having these two females share his pew on Sundays.

And he was beginning to wish they'd share even more.

Mulling that over as they passed through the crowd assembled on the church lawn, he paused to introduce Kristen to a few people. But when he suggested they stop somewhere for lunch, she demurred.

"We had a furniture delivery yesterday while you were at work. I need the rest of the day to assemble some things and get the place in order."

"My bedroom stuff from home came." Beatrice climbed into the truck with his assistance, picking up Kristen's story. "We're going to put it all together this afternoon."

Once Beatrice was settled, he turned to

the woman beside him. "Could you use a hand?"

She bit her lower lip, telling him she was tempted, but in the end she shook her head. "Thanks. I think we'll be okay. The movers already did a lot. Besides, it's your day off."

Dusting off his most persuasive dating-game smile—the one he'd last used years ago on Lisa—he propped a shoulder against the truck door and folded his arms over his chest. "If I don't help you, I'll end up chopping trees on the trail at The Point. Besides, I have to admit my altruism had an ulterior motive. I'm hoping you might reward me by sharing whatever you baked last night. The aroma was driving me crazy."

"Ginger cookies." Beatrice leaned forward from her seat to join the conversation. "They're real good. But we made them for you, anyway, to thank you for inviting us on the hike yesterday."

"That's right." Kristen flexed her fingers on the strap of her purse. "There's a whole plate of them for you on my kitchen counter. I was going to bring them down this afternoon."

"I'll save you the trip and come up. And while I'm there, I'll move a few pieces of furniture. Deal?"

A smile teased the corners of her mouth. "You drive a hard bargain."

"Anything to get my hands on those famous ginger cookies ASAP. My mouth's been watering since you tried to bribe me with them when you wanted to rent the apartment."

Her lips softened into a full-fledged smile. "I think I'm getting the best end of this deal."

"Not if those cookies are half as good as you promised."

"They're yummy," Beatrice pronounced.

"Sold. Let's not waste another minute." With a hand under her elbow, he gave Kristen a boost into the truck.

Once she was settled, he closed the door and took his seat behind the wheel. He'd been hoping to extend this morning's church outing, and while assembling furniture wasn't high on his list of favorite activities, he was nevertheless looking forward to the afternoon.

Because when he was with Kristen, his heart was lighter...no matter what he was doing.

Snapping his seat belt closed, he analyzed that reaction—and came to the obvious conclusion.

If he wasn't careful, he was going to find himself falling head over heels for his tenant.

And truth be told, that prospect was becoming more and more appealing with each passing day.

"Can we put that picture on the wall between the windows?" Beatrice pointed to the spot.

Clint hefted the Disney poster of Ariel from *The Little Mermaid* and gave a mock bow. "Your wish is my command, fair lady."

As he ran a stud finder over the drywall,

Kristen observed from the doorway. She'd shipped every single item from her daughter's room, and they'd re-created it as best they could, given the smaller size and different window configuration.

But all the essentials were in place—pink comforter, gauzy curtains with a matching mock canopy above the bed, white furniture, toy chest and an array of pictures that included the one Beatrice had been keeping in her backpack, of her with her parents on a family vacation at the beach. Until today, she'd only taken it out when she cried herself to sleep at night. More than once Kristen had found the little girl slumbering, her arms wrapped around the frame as she hugged it to her chest.

The photo was now front and center on her nightstand, next to the Disney princess lamp.

As for all the things Kristen had bought on her whirlwind shopping trip before she'd left for Denver—the Cinderella bedspread, the stuffed animals and the fairy princess posters—they'd been relegated to a large discard pile on the floor by the door.

At least she'd tried.

As she stood there, Beatrice came over, rooted through the pile and extracted one of the posters. "Can you hang this over there?" She indicated a bare spot on the wall by the closet as she addressed Clint.

Beatrice hadn't rejected everything she'd bought, after all. For some reason, that small gesture made Kristen feel better.

"Sure thing." Clint took the framed poster, pausing to give her a quick inspection over Beatrice's head. "Everything okay?"

The man had an uncanny ability to sense moods.

Kristen forced her lips into a smile. "Fine. And thanks for doing all this." She gestured around the room. "It would have taken me hours."

"No problem." He continued to work as he spoke. "Small repayment for those great cookies."

Since he'd scarfed down half a dozen al-

ready, she took his praise at face value—
and made a mental note to bake another
batch for him soon.

Pushing off from the doorframe, she
wiped her palms down her slacks and
smiled at Beatrice, who was sitting in the
middle of her bed taking in the familiar
objects that perhaps, at last, would help
her feel at home and keep her from crying
herself to sleep at night.

"I have a surprise for you, honey. Wait
there."

Leaving Clint to finish up, she walked
down the short hall to her room, pulled a
photo album out from under her bed and
ran her fingers over the cover. She didn't
know if a child psychologist would approve
of her version of grief management, and
she prayed the outcome would be positive,
not negative. But Beatrice had clung to the
family album she'd brought with her from
Denver, spending hours paging through it;
this might give her an added measure of
comfort.

Album under her arm, she retraced her

steps and sat on the bed next to her daughter as Clint began collecting his tools.

"When I was in your house in Denver, before the movers came, I took some photos. After I got back here, I had prints made and put them together in this album for you so you could always remember the house you shared with your...mom and dad."

Kristen set the book in Beatrice's lap. The cover featured an eight-by-ten picture of the front of the two-story brick colonial, and for a long moment her daughter examined it. Then slowly she began to turn the pages.

Beatrice scrutinized the entire book in silence, her expression solemn. Kristen had tried to capture all the rooms—and the yard—from various angles, so her daughter would have a photographic record of every nook and cranny of the place she'd called home with the parents she'd loved. But as the minutes ticked by, Kristen's stomach knotted. Maybe she'd made a mistake. Maybe she should have let her daughter's memories recede. Maybe she...

A sudden hand on her shoulder interrupted her panicked thoughts, and she looked up to find Clint watching her. The tenderness in his eyes warmed the cold place deep in her heart, and she exhaled. Mistake or not, he recognized that her intentions had been good.

Beside her, Beatrice closed the book, hugged it to her chest and lifted her chin. Her eyes were shimmering. "Thank you for doing this. I was afraid I was going to forget everything. Now I can remember it for always."

Her daughter's words, along with the comforting squeeze on her shoulder, reassured her she hadn't made a mistake, after all.

And half an hour later, as she walked Clint to the door while Beatrice sat on her bed hugging her Raggedy Ann doll and paging again through both her albums, he reaffirmed that.

"That was a very nice thing to do."

She lifted one shoulder as she followed him out to the landing. "It didn't take much effort. And can you imagine how traumatic it would be to have your whole world turned upside down like that, then find yourself in a new place where everyone is a stranger?"

He studied her, juggling the plate of cookies in one hand and his toolbox in the other, a shaft of pain darkening his blue irises to cobalt. "Yeah. As a matter of fact, I can."

Not the response she'd expected.

But before she could follow up, he changed the subject. "You're doing okay with her, Kristen. She'll come around once she gets to know you better. She just needs time to grieve and adjust."

He wasn't going to explain that enigmatic remark. And after all he'd done for her, she couldn't put him on the spot by probing.

Yet as they said their goodbyes and she thanked him again, she couldn't help but wonder if Genevieve's theory was correct.

Maybe Clint did have an unhappy romance in his past.

Or had some other tragic secret driven him across the country, away from his family?

He disappeared around the corner of the house without a backward glance, and Kristen wandered back inside, shutting the door behind her. If her landlord didn't want to talk, so be it. She had enough problems on her plate without adding speculation—and worry—about him to the mix.

Except there was one small problem.

Clint Nolan was fast becoming far more than a landlord, despite her diligent efforts to keep romance at bay.

And in light of that, her worry and speculation weren't likely to dissipate until she got the answers he didn't seem willing to give.

As Lindsey tallied up the grocery bill, Kristen dug out her credit card and passed it over the high, polished wood counter at the Mercantile. "How's business?"

"Much better since the inn opened." Lindsey slid the card through the scanner and handed it back. "You must be sending guests our way."

Kristen slipped the piece of plastic back in her wallet and signed the receipt, keeping one eye on Beatrice, who was examining the case of frozen treats. "Starfish Bay has a lot to offer—ambience, charm, history. The guests love it."

"I hear business is up at the Orchid, too. And Janice at the art gallery is ecstatic. She's already sold a couple of pricey paintings. Even Jaz says he's been getting more customers."

"I have to be careful about who I send there, though, despite the great food."

Lindsey chuckled. "I hear you."

Turning, Kristen summoned Beatrice, who trotted over.

"What kind of cookies do you have today?" Her daughter examined the latest home-baked offering under the glass dome on the counter.

"Chocolate chip, my husband's favorite. You've had them before." Lindsey rested her forearms on the counter and clasped her hands, leaning over to smile at Beatrice. "Would you like to take one home for dessert? My treat?" She started to reach for a bag.

"No, thank you. We're going to bake cookies tonight. My—" she hesitated and shot Kristen an uncertain look "—my birth mother makes yummy ginger cookies. But Clint ate most of the ones we baked last weekend."

"Did he, now?" Lindsey shifted her attention to Kristen.

Fighting back a blush, Kristen dropped her chin and rummaged through her purse for her keys. "I made them as a thank-you after he helped me assemble some furniture last weekend."

"How neighborly."

She heard the amusement in Lindsey's voice—and knew without looking there was a smirk on her face.

"We had some left, but he's been coming over at night when we feed Clyde, and he ate the rest of them then."

"Clyde?"

"The kitten we feed."

"Clint allows animals in the apartment?" Lindsey arched an eyebrow at Kristen. "He wouldn't even let the Clarks bring their dog when they moved in. After the massive renovation he did on the place, he said he wasn't going to risk any pet damage with tenants."

"No. We're following the rules." Kristen's fingers closed over the keys and she pulled them out. "We feed the cat on the landing."

"Clint sits with us, though. We talk and eat cookies while we wait for Clyde."

"Sounds very cozy."

Kristen picked up her bag of groceries, took Beatrice's hand and urged her toward the door. Of all times for her daughter to get chatty. "See you soon, Lindsey."

"I'll look forward to it. I always enjoy our conversations." The woman's chortle followed them as Kristen pushed through the door to the cheery jingle of the overhead bell.

Beatrice followed in silence until they

reached the car. Then, instead of climbing into her seat, she sent her an uncertain look. "Are you mad at me?"

Frowning, Kristen deposited the grocery bag and her purse on the backseat, shut the door and gave Beatrice her full attention. "Of course not, honey. Why would you think that?"

The little girl scuffed her toe. "Your face got kind of red in there, after I called you my birth mother. I thought maybe you didn't want people to know that or something."

"Oh, Beatrice." Kristen pulled the child into her arms. For once, she didn't resist. "I was blushing for a reason that had nothing to do with you. And it's fine for you to call me your birth mother. That's what I am, and everyone in Starfish Bay knows that."

"But what am I supposed to call you when it's just us?"

At the muffled question, Kristen closed her eyes. How dumb could she be? She'd introduced herself to Beatrice by her first name in Denver, but in all the upheaval since, they'd never settled on a name for her daughter to call her.

"Mom" was out. She already knew that.

Thinking fast, Kristen backed off and stroked her daughter's hair. "Well, you call Clint by his first name. Would you like to call me Kristen?"

Beatrice wrinkled her nose. "Clint is different. He's my friend."

"Maybe I could be your friend, too." At the skeptical narrowing of her daughter's eyes, she quickly tacked on a caveat. "Someday. In the meantime, how about Aunt Kristen?"

"You're not my aunt."

"True. But that would let everyone know we're related. And we can always change it later if we want to."

"Aunt Kristen." Beatrice tried out the title, tipped her head and nodded. "I guess that's okay." She climbed into the car, subject closed.

But as Kristen shut the door and took her place behind the wheel, she couldn't help wishing Beatrice would find it in her heart to call her "Mom."

And perhaps if she tried very hard, if she did everything in her power to earn that title, that was one wish that might come true in Starfish Bay.

Someday.

Chapter Thirteen

Clint rounded the last curve on the trail through the nature preserve, pausing as the woods merged into the manicured grounds of Inn at The Point. Despite the town's reservations about the project, Mattson had done a fine job with the understated resort, blending it into the landscape rather than letting it dominate the scene. The reconstruction of Starfish Bay Chapel, set in its own tiny garden, had been the icing on the cake when it came to selling the plan to the many dubious residents.

His gaze lingered on the small structure, with its soaring white steeple, then traveled on to the stone bench beside it, which offered an unobstructed vista of the sea.

His destination on this Friday afternoon.

Fingering the unopened envelope in his pocket, he crossed the headland. Reading a letter from Lisa hadn't been in the plans for his day off, but there was no sense delaying it. He'd known her note was coming—and was as prepared as he could be for whatever she might have to say.

The sun had dropped past its high point and was beginning its slow descent toward the horizon as he sat on the weathered bench. Below, out of sight, he could hear the waves crashing on the rocks, along with the occasional bark of a seal. Now and then a fine mist drifted up from the turbulent water, dissipating before it reached him.

He hoped the letter would tell him the same was true of Lisa's antipathy.

Taking a fortifying breath, he pulled out the envelope with the familiar handwriting and used his pocketknife to slit the flap. After withdrawing the single sheet of folded paper, he opened it and began to read.

Dear Clint,

Thank you for allowing your father to pass on your address. I know he's already shared the news of my engagement, as I asked him to. I thought it might be easier for you, coming from him. But there was more I needed to say. Hence, this letter.

Over the past three years, I've had a lot of time to think about the tragic day that marked the end of many things. And I've come to realize that putting all the blame on you was grossly unfair. Mistakes happen in tense situations. My father himself said that on many occasions. Humans aren't perfect, especially when under stress. I know you did the best you could under the circumstances.

At the time, though, I was too consumed by grief to see that. Whenever I looked at you, the horror of that day came back to me with suffocating intensity. I needed to hate someone, to blame someone, to find a scapegoat for my anger, and I chose you— for obvious if unjustified reasons.

But I've let the anger and hate go, and I wanted you to know that.

If you still feel you bear any fault for what happened, please know I forgive you. And I ask your forgiveness for holding you in such rancor for so long, and for the terrible things I said to you three years ago. My most heartfelt wish is that you find, or have already found, someone new to love, as I have.

It was signed "All the best," followed by Lisa's sprawling signature.

Clint read the letter through again, bracing for the familiar wave of depression that typically washed over him whenever he thought about his failed romance.

It didn't come.

He frowned, weighing the letter in his hand. Had he learned of Lisa's engagement even a few months ago, he would have been crushed. Yet now he experienced only a sense of closure. He was grateful for her forgiveness, even if it was undeserved. But more than that, he felt relief—and release. As if he'd been set free to move on with his life, unencumbered by the past.

Funny.

Once upon a time, he hadn't been able to envision a future without Lisa.

Now he could.

Thanks in large part to the woman who'd moved into his rental unit—and his heart.

As Clint inhaled a lungful of the tangy salt air and watched a gull wheel overhead, held aloft by unseen wind currents, he was struck by the symbolism. That was kind of how love worked. It sustained you and gave you the courage to soar.

And that brought him back to Kristen.

It was too soon to apply the *L* word to his lovely tenant. If he'd learned one thing from his experience with Lisa, it was to take things slow and easy. Besides, while Kristen had been honest with him about her mistakes, he'd never shared his past with her. How would she react to the story that had sent him on a cross-country flight? Would she accept his mistakes as a human failing, the way Lisa ultimately had...or view them the way he did—as the cause of a tragedy that could have been averted?

Clint didn't know. But if he wanted to take his relationship with Kristen to the next level, he needed to find out.

Sooner rather than later.

Kristen stepped out of Starfish Bay Chapel, pulled the door shut behind her and turned the key in the lock. Everything was prepped for her meeting with a prospective bride and groom later this afternoon.

And it couldn't come soon enough. She was ready for this week to be over.

Except the weekend didn't promise to be any less busy.

Pocketing the key in her suit jacket, she sighed. Tomorrow she had to run her car in to the dealer in Eureka to have the technician check out a funny noise. After that she had an appointment for Beatrice with a pediatrician. Her daughter didn't need a checkup, but she wanted her on a local doctor's patient roster just in case. Grocery shopping rounded out her agenda.

Their Sunday-morning trip to church with Clint, however…that was something to look forward to.

She smiled as she walked through the tiny garden, stopping to smell a flower she didn't recognize. Those couple of hours at church would be the bright spot of her weekend—because of both the man who'd suggested it and the sense of peace she'd found there last week.

Reaching the end of the garden, she opened the white picket gate, exited… and hesitated. In light of her hectic day so far, it would be nice to sit on the weathered stone bench off to the side and enjoy a moment of tranquillity before the bride and groom descended. With a quick check of her watch, she made her decision. She could spare a few minutes.

After closing the gate, she walked to the

right instead of the left, her shoes silent on the carpet of grass. But seconds later she pulled up short.

The bench was already occupied—by the very man she'd just been thinking about.

Curious, she edged closer. Clint was looking out to sea, only a portion of his strong profile visible, and he had a sheet of paper in his hand.

Her step faltered. The scene had a contemplative feel about it, as if he'd come here to find an oasis of quiet and solitude. Perhaps she should retreat, leave him to...

All at once, as if sensing her presence, he angled toward her...and took the decision out of her hands.

Rising, he gave her a slow smile. "Hi."

"Hi yourself." She continued toward him, but stopped several feet away, planning a quick escape. "I'd accuse you of trespassing, but I understand that bench belongs to the town."

"It does. Lindsey fought hard for it. I think it has special significance for her and Nate, from when they were kids." He gestured to it. "Would you like to join me for a few minutes?"

She eyed the sheet of paper in his hand. "I don't want to intrude."

He looked down, as if he'd forgotten he was holding anything, and tucked it into the pocket of his shirt. "You're not."

Since he seemed sincere, she crossed to the bench. "All right. The bride and groom won't be here for a few minutes."

"There's a wedding today?"

She smiled and claimed the far side of the bench. "No. They're thinking about having a destination wedding here. I'm going to show them around and do a sell job."

"I have a feeling this place sells itself."

"For the most part." She braced her palms on the seat and leaned back, letting the sun warm her face. "So how come you're not at work?"

"I have to do a couple of special programs tomorrow and Sunday afternoon. When I work weekends, I get a day off during the week."

"And you decided to spend it at The Point?"

He didn't respond at once, and Kristen opened her eyes to find him watching her. His enigmatic expression kicked her pulse up a notch, and she straightened at the odd vibes wafting her way. "What's wrong?"

Instead of answering that question, he withdrew the folded sheet of paper from his pocket again and responded to her previous comment. "I came out here because of this."

Kristen sized up the thick, expensive, cream-colored stock. It was personal stationery—suggesting a personal letter.

"From a friend?" Her query was cautious but receptive. If he wanted to talk, fine. But she wasn't going to push—and perhaps push him away.

"More than a friend, at one time." He fingered the letter. "Lisa was my fiancée. We broke up three years ago."

Fiancée.

Clint had been engaged before he came to Starfish Bay.

So Genevieve had been right all along. Clint did have an unhappy romance in his past.

Had he been engaged to the woman whose photo was still in his wallet? The woman who, from the quick glimpse she'd gotten at Jaz's, bore a remarkable resemblance to her? The woman whose identity she'd wondered about more nights than she cared to recall as she tried to fall asleep?

"I'm sorry." It was a lame response, but what else was there to say?

"I was, too, at the time. Not so much anymore." He tucked the letter back in his pocket. "Thanks to you."

At his candor, a flutter of excitement rippled along her nerve endings. But close on its heels came another ripple—this one prompted by apprehension. Even though she was happy he seemed to have moved past his broken engagement and was interested in her, the only relationship she had time to cultivate at the moment was the one with her daughter.

"Clint, I…"

He lifted a hand to cut her off. "I'm not trying to rush you into anything. I know you're still grappling with a lot of issues, and Beatrice is your first priority. That's as it should be. Besides, once you know my story, you may not want to have anything to do with me, anyway."

"I find that hard to believe."

"Believe it. I've made a lot of mistakes."

"And I haven't?"

"Some mistakes are more serious than others." His Adam's apple bobbed, and when he continued, his voice had hoarsened. "Someone died because of mine."

Only the muted crash of the surf at the base of the headland broke the silence as Kristen searched the depths of Clint's blue eyes. The same guilt, shame and self-reproach that had burdened her soul for nine years was reflected back at her.

"Do you want to tell me about it?"

He grimaced. "My ego says no. But my ego is what got me in trouble in the past, and I'm not going there again. It's only fair that I share my story with you, just as you shared yours with me. Assuming you want to hear it, of course."

"Yes. I do." Her words came out sure and strong, and she scooted closer to emphasize her next point. "Whatever you tell me isn't going to change my opinion of you."

"Don't be so certain."

She let that go. He'd find out the truth of her statement soon enough. "I assume the letter is related to this."

"Yeah." A spasm of pain tightened his features, and he wrapped his fingers around the edges of the bench. "She wanted me to know she's forgiven me."

"For breaking up?"

"No." A beat of silence ticked by. "For killing her father."

The breath whooshed out of Kristen's lungs as his shocking words echoed in the quiet air. She tried to process them, but her brain short-circuited.

Clint had killed his fiancée's father?

It didn't compute.

But she did begin to get an inkling of why he'd fled cross-country.

Can you imagine how traumatic it would be to have your whole world turned upside down, then find yourself in a new place where everyone is a stranger?

She'd said that to him days ago, in reference to Beatrice.

Now she understood his response.

He turned to her, apology in his eyes. "Sorry. I probably should have led up to that rather than dump it in your lap all at once."

Get a grip, Kristen. Say something. Anything.

"What happened?" Folding her hands into a tight ball in her lap, she choked out the words.

He looked back out over the shimmering sea. "Lisa's father was a cop, too. One day, a disgruntled ex-employee of an electronics firm took his former boss and several other employees hostage. Lisa's father was one of the first responders, and the gunman shot him in the arm and took him hostage, too.

"The cops surrounded the building, a negotiator was brought in, and the SWAT team was mobilized in case the situation degenerated to a tactical resolution. I was a sniper on the team. A real hotshot. I had the best shooting record of anyone—on targets, anyway." He gave a disparaging snort, disgust twisting his features. "Real life is different, however, as I found out."

Clint paused, his gaze fixed on the distant horizon. Though he remained motionless, Kristen could feel the almost palpable tension in his body, and drops of sweat beaded on his upper lip.

"My supervisor knew Lisa and I were engaged. So despite my stellar shooting record, he gave me the option to pass the sniper duty to someone else. I turned him down. I told him I was a pro, that I wouldn't let my personal feelings get in the way of doing the job—if it needed to be done. And that was a long shot. Tactical resolutions are the exception rather than the rule.

"But nothing followed the rules that day. Negotiations fell apart. The gunman became more agitated. He demanded that a helicopter land in the parking lot and pick him up, along with one of the hostages. The plan was for a sniper to take him out as he crossed the lot toward the helicopter."

"Your fiancée's father was the hostage he took to the helicopter?" Kristen leaned toward him as the horror of the situation began to fully register.

"He ended up taking two hostages. Lisa's father, who was already injured, and a young woman employee. He had one on each side, to shield him. What he didn't know was that two snipers were positioned on the upper floors of nearby buildings. Me and one of my buddies. But it was clear from the instant he came out that I had the best line of sight. Neither was optimal, though, with hostages in such close proximity."

All at once, Clint stood and moved a few steps closer to the edge of the cliff, keeping his face averted as he continued.

"I settled in, lined the guy up in my crosshairs—and started to sweat. Badly.

That had never happened to me before. I was always cool and in control in training, but now I was a flex of the finger away from ending someone's life. And if my aim was off an nth of a degree, I could hit one of the hostages instead—including my future father-in-law."

"I didn't think snipers were used if there was serious danger of hitting an innocent party." Kristen dug deep to dredge up her meager knowledge of police procedure.

"They aren't." Clint's tone flattened. "But Lisa's father was a veteran on the force. He would have known what was happening with the SWAT team. We were counting on him to create some sort of diversion that would give us an opening."

"Did he?"

"Yeah. Halfway to the helicopter, he stumbled and went down on one knee, like he'd tripped. I had a clear shot for about two seconds, but I was so busy second-guessing myself I didn't respond fast enough. By the time I pulled the trigger, the gunman was yanking Lisa's father back to his feet. My bullet went through his aorta."

Kristen sucked in a sharp breath. Closed her eyes. Fought back a wave of nausea. "Oh, Clint." She rose and took a step toward him, but his rigid stance sent a clear *keep away* message, just as Beatrice's often did.

"He died on the spot." Clint continued as if she hadn't spoken, his voice ragged. "In the chaos that followed, the other sniper got off a shot and took the gunman out. But it was too late for Lisa's father."

"And she blamed you for his death."

Clint swung toward her, lines of strain etched on his face. "Wouldn't you?"

She stared at him, thinking about how much she'd loved her own father. How a piece of her heart had died each day as she'd watched the disease ravage his once-robust body. How she'd hated the cancer with every ounce of her being. How she'd needed someone to blame—and chose God.

Hate was a powerful emotion…and

blame was a common coping mechanism. She could understand how his fiancée had felt.

Yet knowing Clint even for these few short weeks, she couldn't imagine herself hating him—or blaming him.

"I don't think so." She said the words slowly, still working through all he'd told her. "It was just a tragic, horrible situation. And people are human. They make mistakes. I know that firsthand. Plus, you were under incredible stress."

He raked his fingers through his hair, and the sun glinted off a few specks of silver she'd never noticed before. Visible evidence of his trauma, perhaps?

But what of the invisible evidence?

Her heart ached for him.

"Lisa finally came to the same conclusion. That's what this letter is about." He tapped his shirt pocket. "But I don't deserve her absolution. What happened that day *was* my fault. I was trained to handle that kind of stress. Every sniper was. Yet I choked. At the very first niggle of doubt—

and I had more than one as the situation escalated—I should have stepped back. But my ego and pride got in the way. And because of that her father died."

His shoulders drooped and he clenched his hands into fists. When he continued, his tone was subdued. "I've prayed for mercy, and I believe God has forgiven me. I'm grateful Lisa has, too, but I know what happened was my fault, and I still wrestle with the guilt. I suspect I always will."

"Guilt can be hard to shake." She lowered herself back to the bench, running a finger over the rough edge. "I guess all you can do is learn from your mistakes and know that if the same situation came up again, you'd make a different choice."

"Like you did." Regret pooled in his eyes. "I envy you your second chance."

Was he talking about the sniper situation? His ex-fiancée? Both?

She gestured toward his pocket. "If she's forgiven you, maybe she'd be willing to try again."

"Not likely. She just got engaged."

"Oh." Kristen tried not to be pleased about that. She should be consoling Clint, not thinking about her own future. "I'm sorry."

"I'm not. I'm happy for her."

She studied him, searching for any sign of insincerity, but found none. "I thought maybe… I mean, you still have her picture in your wallet, don't you?" Now that she'd heard his story, who else could the mystery woman be?

"Not since that day we went to Jaz's— long before I knew she'd met someone new." He took a step toward her. "I'm going to tell you something I haven't shared with anyone else. In hindsight, I'm not certain Lisa and I were the best match. She was a corporate attorney, very much into big-city living. I like the outdoors and small-town life."

"So what attracted you to each other?"

He shrugged. "I was bowled over by her polish when her father introduced us, and I guess she saw some appealing qualities in me. Don't get me wrong. She's a lovely person, and we had some good times, but our interests and priorities were different. I realize now that could have caused problems down the road."

"We look a lot alike, though, don't we?"

"Yes."

"How do you feel about that?" Might as well ask the question. It would eat away at her if she didn't.

"Honestly? It was a bit off-putting to me when we met. But as I've discovered, those similarities are superficial." He took another step toward her, but stopped as a shadow of uncertainty darkened his eyes. "As long as we're being honest, I might as well lay everything on the table. The truth is, you're becoming very important to me. I understand, though, if this story changes any feelings you might have for me."

She rose to face him, recalling the day she'd laid her own past before this man, assuming he'd judge her and find her wanting. Instead, he'd surprised her by his willingness to put a better spin on the situation than she ever had, and by acknowledging her mistakes without condemning her.

Perhaps she could do the same for him.

Wiping her palms on her skirt, she closed the distance between them, reached for his hand and twined her fingers with his. "I didn't know you three years ago. Maybe you were a hotshot. Maybe your ego was too big. Maybe you could have changed that outcome by stepping back. Then again, maybe not. All I know for sure is that I respect and admire the man you are today."

A sheen appeared in his eyes, and he squeezed her fingers. "Thank you."

Without releasing her hand, he lifted his other arm—as if he intended to touch her cheek.

Her lungs stalled.

Her heart tripped into double time.

She leaned toward him expectantly…

All at once the jarring ring of the cell phone in her pocket shattered the stillness—and the mood.

He dropped his hand, leaving her disappointed…and filled with a yearning so strong it scared her.

"Sorry." She mumbled the apology and fumbled for the phone with shaky fingers. "Yes?"

"It's Steve. There's a couple here at the front desk who said they have an appointment with you for a wedding consultation."

She checked her watch. Talk about losing track of time. She was ten minutes late. "Tell them I'm on my way." After pressing the end button, she slid the phone back into her pocket.

"Your bride and groom?"

"Yes. I have to go."

"I understand. It's a workday for you." He shoved his hands in his pockets and took a step back.

She hesitated. Was his retreat symbolic? Did he regret the confidences he'd shared—and the almost-touch he'd initiated? Or was he just trying to give her some space after his dramatic revelation?

With potential clients waiting, she didn't have time to explore those questions…but neither did she intend to walk away leaving any doubts about her feelings.

She took two deliberate steps toward him. "I want you to know I appreciate everything you shared with me today. And you're becoming important to me, too. What you said at the beginning, about Beatrice being my top priority for now, is true. But for the record, I'm interested in seeing where things might lead when the time *is* right. Assuming you're willing to wait."

Some of the tautness in his features softened. "Patience has never been my strong suit, but I'll cultivate it for you."

Her heart warmed at his husky comment, and she smiled. "That's nice to know. And now I need to deal with someone else's romance." She gestured toward the chapel as her phone rang again. With an apologetic glance and wave, she pulled it out of her pocket and started back toward the inn.

But as she talked with Mark Stephens about possible activities for a large party that would be checking in the following week, she took a quick look over her shoulder.

Clint was still standing on the edge of the precipice, the blue sea sparkling behind his broad shoulders, the sun warming his bronzed skin, the fine mist from the surf rising behind him.

He looked like the hero from a romance novel.

Normally, Kristen would squelch such a fanciful notion. Dismiss it as the stuff of fairy tales.

But today, she indulged herself.

Because thanks to a tall, dark and handsome ranger, she was beginning to believe that maybe…just maybe…happy endings weren't found only in storybooks.

And that dreams really could come true in Starfish Bay.

Chapter Fourteen

"I missed Clint at church today."

As Beatrice's comment floated back to her on the needle-carpeted trail, Kristen hefted her daypack into a more comfortable position. "I did, too, honey." *A lot.* "But when someone calls in sick at work, other people have to fill in. He promised to stop by tonight for some cookies, though."

"That will be fun. I like how we all sit on the steps and wait for Clyde and talk." Beatrice stopped and squatted beside the trail. "Look. A banana slug."

Kristen closed the distance between them and dropped to one knee. Unlike most of the forest creatures, the bright yellow slug made no attempt to blend in with its surroundings. "They're very colorful, aren't they?"

"Yeah." Beatrice looked over at her and fingered the tie on her hooded sweater. "Thank you for bringing me on this hike, Aunt Kristen."

She smiled and put her arm around the girl's shoulders. "I like this place, too. It's always quiet and peaceful here."

"But the sunbeams went away."

Kristen surveyed the forest. She'd been deep in thought during the entire hike, giving Beatrice perfunctory answers to her questions as she mulled over all Clint had told her on Friday. Although the day had been sunny when they'd left the parking area, now the late-afternoon light had dimmed. High above their heads, wisps of fog swirled around the branches of the towering trees. As she watched, the tendrils dipped lower, like the tentacles of an octopus.

A shiver rippled through her.

"You're right, honey." She stood and glanced at her watch. Had they been hiking for an hour? She should have kept closer track of the time—and the weather. Northern California fog could be treacherous.

Stomach clenching, she tightened her grip on the straps of her daypack. "I think we'd better start back."

"But we haven't come to the end of the trail yet."

"There isn't really an end. It joins up with other trails. Most people just walk until they get tired, then follow the same path back. Remember, we still have to make cookies when we get home. I have a new recipe called double-chocolate fudge delights for us to try." Since her repertoire was limited, the pastry chef at the inn had taken pity on her and shared one of his recipes. Fortunately, it sounded simple and straightforward.

"I bet I'll like those."

"I bet you will, too."

Beatrice started to retrace their route

without further protest. "I'm getting kind of hungry anyway."

"Would you like a granola bar?"

Her daughter gave her a get-real look over her shoulder. "Yuck."

"It's not bad. I bet you'd like the apple-cinnamon flavor." But truth be told, it wasn't as appealing as cookies or a peanut butter and jelly sandwich, two of the things her daughter never passed up. Kristen made a mental note to replace her standard daypack fare with more appealing treats. Now that Beatrice's appetite had begun to pick up, she was always hungry. Kids, it seemed, were bottomless pits.

"No, thank you."

Kristen didn't push. She wasn't a huge fan of granola bars, either.

For the next ten minutes, as they walked in silence, Kristen kept an eye on the descending fog. A few swirls were now blowing across the path, and a damp chill began to seep through her sweater.

They needed to pick up the pace.

But first, they needed to put on their waterproof jackets.

"Beatrice, wait up." She stopped and slipped the pack off her shoulders.

Her daughter trotted back to join her. "What's wrong?"

"It's a little chilly now, with the sun gone. I think we should put on our jackets. Pull up your hood, too."

She dug the smaller slicker out and handed it to Beatrice, then slid her arms into her own.

"How come it's getting dark?" Beatrice surveyed the hilly, fern-covered terrain with a frown as she tugged the hood into place. "Isn't it too early for that?"

"Oh, it's always darker in a forest with such tall trees." Kristen tried to sound casual, despite her own worry. Beatrice was right. It was far too dark for four o'clock.

"It's kind of scary with the fog and all." Beatrice edged closer, a touch of trepidation in her voice.

Kristen agreed. But she didn't intend to

tell that to her daughter. The youngster was already spooked.

Forcing her lips into a smile, she adopted a lighthearted tone. "I don't know. It kind of reminds me of Brigadoon."

"What's Brigadoon?"

"You've never heard of Brigadoon?" She took Beatrice's hand and resumed walking as fast as the child's shorter legs could manage. Even with the accelerated speed, she figured they were forty minutes from the trailhead.

"No. Is it a place?"

"A very magical place that appears out of the mist once every hundred years."

As Kristen relayed the tale of the enchanted Scottish town to her enthralled daughter, she tried to quell her growing unease. The fog was continuing to thicken, billowing down from the treetops that had disappeared soon after she'd begun her story. Visibility on the path was decreasing with frightening speed. By the time she wrapped up her narrative, it was down to less than fifteen feet.

"That's a cool story, Aunt Kristen. Do you know any more?"

"Sure. I know lots of stories like that. And I have some real-life stories, too, about when I was growing up on the farm. My brother and I had some great adventures."

"Will you tell me some of those, too? I'd like to hear—"

Beatrice stumbled over a root, and Kristen grabbed her before she fell.

Only then did the thick fog register with her daughter.

"Wow!" The word came out hushed, awed—and scared. "I can hardly see the trail. Are we going to be able to find our way back?"

"Of course." Kristen drew her close, and for once Beatrice didn't resist. "We'll just walk faster and pay extra attention to the edges of the path so we don't wander off."

But a few minutes later, Kristen had to

admit defeat. Despite her diligence, they'd somehow parted company with the trail.

Stopping beside a giant fern, she fought down a wave of panic.

"What's wrong, Aunt Kristen?"

"You know, it's getting kind of hard to see, and I don't want to get lost. I think it might be better if we find a spot to sit and wait for the fog to lift."

"Will it do that before dark?"

Morning fog doesn't usually linger past nine. Afternoon fog...that's a different story. It can last all night.

As Genevieve's comment from her first visit replayed in her memory, her panic surged again. Because in the short time she'd been in Starfish Bay, she'd seen plenty of evidence to support the woman's statement.

They could end up being here all night.

With the mountain lions.

Her heart began to pound.

"Aunt Kristen?" Beatrice plucked at the

sleeve of her slicker. "How long will the fog last?"

It took a second for her daughter's frightened query to register.

"I don't know, honey, but we have food and water and everything we need until the sun comes out again. We'll just have to find somewhere dry to wait."

"Like a big hollowed-out tree trunk?"

"That would work."

"I bet there's one close by."

She hoped so. Beautiful as the forest was with the sun streaming through the treetops, it was downright spooky—and disorienting—in the fog. Any sort of shelter would be welcome.

"Let me get my flashlight and we'll check a few trees." Kristen slipped off her daypack, unzipped it and rummaged around for the flashlight. Once she had it in hand, she clicked it on, slung the pack over one shoulder and reached for her daughter's hand.

Beatrice didn't need to be coaxed. She

tucked her fingers into Kristen's and stuck as close as possible.

The flashlight was of marginal use in the fog, but it did come in handy when the third tree they investigated yielded a small hollowed-out area at the base. It wasn't as roomy as some of the ones Clint had shown the children on the junior rangers hike, but sufficient to accommodate the two of them.

"This should work, don't you think?" Kristen flashed the light around the interior. The ground was dry, and she didn't see lurking spiders or other creepy-crawly creatures.

"I guess so." Her tone dubious, Beatrice peered into the space, still clinging to her hand.

"Before we go inside, let me check my cell phone just in case I have a signal." She pulled it out and flipped it open.

Clint had been right.

No signal.

"Does it work?" Beatrice watched her with wide eyes.

"No, but that's okay. We'll be fine." She tucked it back in her pocket. If she thought any other hikers might be close by, she'd call out. Strength in numbers and all that. But theirs had been the only car at the trailhead. "Should I go in first?"

The little girl nodded and continued to cling to her hand.

Ducking down, Kristen stepped into the tree. Once inside, she could stand. Barely.

Beatrice followed.

"Let's sit over there." Kristen indicated the most protected spot.

After they settled in, she opened her day-pack and took inventory. First-aid kit, compass, matches, digital camera, binoculars, two bottles of water and assorted snacks.

Most of the items were useless—and she hoped she wouldn't need the first-aid kit.

As for the snacks…before long Beatrice might be sufficiently hungry to eat the yucky granola bar. If she stayed calm, it wouldn't take long for her appetite to kick in.

"Okay." Kristen propped her back against the inside of the trunk and pulled Beatrice close beside her. "We're all set. Would you like a drink of water?"

"No."

"Then how about another story? I could tell you about the time my brother and I tried to teach one of our dogs how to fly."

Beatrice wiggled around so she could look up at her in the dim light. "Dogs can't fly."

Kristen smiled and brushed the wispy blond hair back from her daughter's forehead. "That's true. But we thought if we made him a pair of wings, maybe he could learn."

"Did it work?"

"No. And he was not an enthusiastic student."

Kristen launched into the tale, playing up the funny parts, doing her best to keep her daughter entertained. She even elicited a few giggles. And she managed to coax Beatrice to try the granola bar and drink some water.

As for her own appetite, it was nonexistent. She was too busy praying that no stray mountain lion in search of his own dinner would happen upon them.

It was going to be a very long night.

"You better make a fast exit unless you're planning to sleep here."

At his boss's remark, Clint checked out the fog rolling past the window of the visitor center and grabbed his jacket. "No, thanks. I've sacked out here on a few occasions and the accommodations stink."

The man sniggered. "No argument from me. Been there, done that. You want to take the parkway when you leave instead of 101? You could check the trailheads while I shut things down here."

"Sure."

"Let's hope any hikers had the good sense to get out fast when this started to roll in. Otherwise, they'd better be prepared to wait it out."

Clint shoved his arms into his jacket and grabbed his hat, still eyeing the fog. "Yeah. We could be socked in all night."

"No kidding. Drive safe."

With a wave of acknowledgment, Clint exited the center. The fog continued to move in thick and fast as he crossed the lot toward his truck, the gray mist swirling through the deserted parking lot and obscuring the field where the elk liked to gather. At this rate, driving back to Starfish Bay was going to be dicey. That last winding stretch of coastal road leading into town was a bear to drive in bad weather.

Once behind the wheel, Clint tossed his hat onto the passenger seat, started the engine, turned on his fog lights and drove toward the parkway. The faster he got home, the better.

Unfortunately, fast was not an option. Visibility continued to deteriorate at an alarming clip, making it more and more difficult to spot the trailheads or any cars parked beside them. He reduced his speed to a crawl, using his odometer to help him gauge the location of the trails.

So far, the park appeared to be deserted. For once, hikers must have heeded the warning signs of the encroaching fog and…

He slowed, scrutinizing the roadside parking area by the Brown Creek Trail.

Was that a car?

Guiding the truck to the right, he edged closer.

It was a car.

Expelling a sigh, he set the brake and pulled out his radio. His boss picked up as he walked toward the vehicle, and he gave him the bad news. "I've got a car at Brown Creek."

The man said a word that wasn't pretty. "Any sign of the occupants?"

"I'm checking." Clint squinted at the car as he drew close—and sucked in a sharp breath as the make registered. It was a silver Accord.

The kind of car Kristen drove.

He was tempted to repeat the word his boss had used.

"Find anything?" His boss's voice crackled over the radio.

He flashed his light in the windows. Empty—except for a tattered Raggedy Ann doll in the backseat that confirmed his suspicion.

It was Kristen's car.

Meaning she and Beatrice were somewhere on the trail.

He hoped.

In fog like this, it was easy to become disoriented, wander off, get lost—and get hurt.

His pulse kicked up a notch.

"Clint?"

He swallowed past his fear. "It's empty. But I recognize it. It belongs to my neighbor. She must have gone hiking with her daughter."

"Not good." The man's tone was grim. "Let me round up some people to help with the search. I just got a report of a mountain lion sighting from some hikers who were on that trail earlier today. Odds are it was a bobcat, but you never know."

Clint's heart stuttered.

Reminding himself that the threat of a mountain lion attack was statistically very small, he reined in his panic and strode back to his truck. "In the meantime, I'll start a circuit."

"Okay. Stay in touch by radio."

"Will do." He exchanged his regular flashlight for one better equipped to cut through fog and grabbed his backpack—praying he wouldn't need the emergency supplies inside.

After sliding the radio back on his belt, he set off down the trail. Every fifteen seconds, he called Kristen's name.

But as he wound deeper and deeper into the forest, the only response was the hollow, foreboding echo of his voice.

* * *

What time was it?

In the shadowy confines of the tree trunk, Kristen had no idea. And she didn't want to flip on the flashlight to find out. It might wake Beatrice, who was cuddled against her, sound asleep, her stomach full with both of the granola bars plus the baggie of trail mix.

At least one of them was relaxed.

But who knew the quiet daytime forest could be so full of sounds at dusk? Every breaking twig, every rustling branch, sent her pulse skyrocketing.

On top of everything else, the temperature was diving.

Even as she stifled a shiver, Beatrice stirred and spoke in a sleepy voice. "I'm cold, Aunt Kristen."

"We can fix that." Easing away from her daughter, she unzipped her slicker and shrugged out of it. Then she turned on the flashlight and helped Beatrice into it, checking out the fog as she folded back the sleeves to accommodate her daughter's shorter arms. If anything, it was thicker than ever.

"But this is your coat."

Despite Beatrice's protest, she zipped up the jacket, suppressing another shiver as she spoke. "I'm not cold. And we'll stay real close together. That will help keep us warm. Why don't you climb onto my lap?"

Beatrice complied, snuggling close, and Kristen wrapped her arms around the little girl, savoring this one bright spot in their ill-fated hike. Her back might be cold against the tree trunk, but with her daughter resting against it, her heart was warm.

"Maybe Clint will find us." Beatrice yawned.

It was a nice but futile wish. He wouldn't even know they were missing until he stopped by for cookies and conversation later—and he'd have no idea where they'd gone.

But there was no reason to dash her daughter's hopes.

"You never know. In the meantime, we'll stay snuggled up inside this tree. Won't this be a great adventure to tell Rose about next week?"

"I guess. But you know what? It's more fun to read about adventures in books than to be in a real one."

Kristen leaned her head back and closed her eyes.

No kidding.

As the minutes ticked by and Beatrice's warmth seeped into her, she, too, began to relax and think about other things. Like the precious gift in her arms. The blessing of her rekindling faith. And the special man who was fast winning her heart.

Funny. As she'd begun to make her peace with God over the past few weeks, she'd experienced two emotions long absent from her life: gratitude, and hope for a brighter tomorrow than she'd ever let herself dream of since the day she'd signed away her rights as a mother.

A smile playing on her lips, Kristen exhaled long and slow and let herself drift into a dream starring Clint that offered a welcome escape from both the chilly air and her anxiety.

How much time passed, she had no idea. But a sudden, cold prick on her forehead pulled her abruptly back to reality.

She lifted her hand and felt her temple. It was wet.

Apparently their snug, hollowed-out tree wasn't so snug after all.

As she flexed her foot to try to restore the circulation cut off by her daughter's weight, she peeked through the opening in the tree trunk. Was it her imagination, or had the fog thinned? And was it a bit brighter out, too?

She checked her watch. Seven-thirty. This time of year, they'd have enough daylight left to make it back to the trail-head before dark—assuming they could find their way back to the trail and the fog didn't thicken again.

Both were optimistic assumptions.

But what if they stayed here overnight and the fog was no better—or worse—in the morning?

Besides, she agreed with Beatrice. Adventures were better in books. The thought of spending the night in a tree, surrounded by wild creatures, held no appeal.

Easing away from her daughter, she crawled over to the opening, exited and stood, holding on to the tree for support while the feeling returned to her leg. No question about it. The fog situation had improved. Visibility was now at least ten feet. That was far enough to keep them on the trail…if they could find it.

"Are we leaving, Aunt Kristen?" Beside her, Beatrice poked her head out of the tree.

"I think we might want to give it a try. We can always come back to this tree if we have any trouble finding the trail." She scanned the terrain. "But I don't think we're far from it. Why don't you—"

Fear snatched the words from her mouth.

What had caused that darting shadow at the edge of her visibility?

"Kristen, honey…hand me the flashlight. And get back inside."

"What's wrong?"

"Just hand me the flashlight, okay?"

Kristen kept her gaze fixed on the spot where she'd seen the shadow, waiting for her daughter to find the flashlight. Once it was in her hand, she clicked it on. Swung it in a slow arc.

And felt the scream rising in her throat as the light hit a pair of yellowish-green eyes that were staring directly at her.

Chapter Fifteen

Clint lifted the bottle of water to his lips and took a long swig to lubricate his parched throat. He'd been calling Kristen's name every fifteen seconds for the past twenty minutes, with no response. Had they taken the South Fork spur instead of staying on the Brown Creek Trail? He'd assumed they'd stick to familiar territory, but…

A woman's scream ripped through the air.

Kristen!

He sucked in a breath, choking on the water he'd just swallowed. Gasping, he tossed the bottle aside and took off in the direction of the cry, struggling to breathe.

A child's terrified cry pierced the stillness, vaulting his pulse into overdrive. He veered off the trail toward the sound, crashing through the giant ferns as he opened his mouth to call out.

But Kristen spoke first, yelling so loud there was no chance she'd hear him.

"Stay away, do you hear me? Don't even think about coming closer! Go away! Get out of here! See this stick? If you come any closer, I'm going to take a swing!"

As she continued her loud tirade, he emerged from the fog into a pocket of clear air and sized up the ominous scene in one swift, comprehensive glance.

Twenty feet away, Kristen was standing in front of the hollowed-out base of a redwood. She was gripping a five-foot-long branch with both hands, holding it high as she waved it back and forth.

Crouched less than fifteen feet in front of her was a mountain lion, its stare fixed on her. And it was slowly creeping forward.

The lion was in attack mode.

Kristen was doing all the right things. Shouting, trying to look as tall as she could, maintaining eye contact. She'd obviously read the material he'd given her that first day.

But it wasn't going to work.

The lion was intent on taking down its prey.

Any second, in one short, sudden burst of speed it was going to spring toward Kristen's neck.

As Clint pulled his Sig Sauer from its holster and raised his arm, locking it straight out while steadying the gun with his other hand, the lion made its move.

Bunching its haunches, it leaped, front paws extended.

Without hesitation, he aimed and pulled the trigger.

As the shot echoed through the fog, Kristen screamed and swung at the leaping lion. The branch connected with the flailing animal, but the weight of its limp, falling body threw her off balance. She went down inches from the motionless animal.

Chest heaving, she rolled away. Grabbed the limb she'd dropped. Started to rise.

"Kristen! It's okay." Clint sprinted toward her.

She stared up at him as he approached, still poised to fight, every muscle taut, her knuckles white around the piece of wood.

Once he verified the lion was no longer a threat, he knelt in front of her and did a quick assessment. Her face was white, her eyes were glassy and she was shaking badly.

"Kristen…" He reached over and touched her cold cheek, swallowing past his sudden hoarseness. "It's okay. You're okay. Where's Beatrice?"

"I—I'm back here."

He pivoted to find the little girl peeking out from inside the tree. She was enveloped in Kristen's yellow slicker, her complexion as colorless as her mother's.

"Are you hurt?"

"N-no. Can I c-come out now?"

"Yes. Stand by me, okay?"

The child approached him, making a wide circle around the mountain lion. "Is Aunt Kristen all right?"

"She will be." He turned his attention back to the woman crouched in front of him and tried to pry the limb out of her hands. She wouldn't relinquish her grip. He got up close to her, forcing her to focus on him. "Kristen, it's okay. You can let go. The mountain lion is dead." He spoke the words slowly, his gaze locked on hers.

She blinked, and her eyes began to clear. But as they did, her shaking intensified and she choked out a sob. "Beatrice…"

"Is right here." Clint drew the little girl forward.

"Thank You, God!" Kristen pulled her into a fierce hug.

That was when Clint noticed the tear in the sleeve of her sweater.

And the blood.

Easing Beatrice back, he leaned closer to examine the two deep scratches on Kristen's forearm.

Claw marks.

From an animal that had a strong chance of being rabid.

Only a mountain lion that was very sick or very hungry would risk attacking an adult human. Usually they went out of their way to avoid people and remain invisible.

He took a deep breath and sent a silent prayer heavenward. *Please, Lord, spare her that. With everything else she's dealing with, she doesn't need a painful series of shots.*

"He must have clipped you as he fell." As he spoke he pulled his radio off his belt with one hand and lowered his backpack to the ground with the other. Working it open, he continued in a tone he hoped sounded more calm than he felt. "You might need a few stitches. Let me put in an emergency call and then I'll do some preliminary cleanup."

The radio crackled to life, and he gave his boss a quick recap. "We're going to need to get the animal tested right away."

"You've got injuries?"

"A minor maul."

"Do you need me to send in paramedics or have an ambulance dispatched?"

"No." Kristen was focused on her daughter as she responded, and somehow she summoned up a shaky smile for the frightened little girl as she took her hand. "I'll walk out. That won't be a problem."

Clint wasn't as certain of that, but he understood her reasoning. Beatrice had been traumatized by the incident, too. The lower-key they could play this, the better. And she could lean on him.

As much as she needed to.

For as long as she needed to.

"No." He spoke into the radio. "We'll come out on our own and I'll drive her to the hospital in Eureka myself."

"Okay. Give me a location on the lion and I'll get someone in there in less than thirty minutes."

As Clint complied, he kept an eye on Kristen. Her shaking hadn't subsided, nor had her pallor abated. Her respiration was also shallow.

She was on the verge of shock.

He ended the call as quickly as he could, then opened his first-aid kit.

"Wow. That puts mine to shame." She tried to joke, but couldn't quite pull it off.

"Beatrice, honey, would you sit behind Kristen and unwrap this for me?" He removed a Mylar blanket and handed it to her. "And open this too, please." He passed her a PowerBar. While those tasks did need to be done, he was more interested in keeping her occupied while he examined Kristen's scratches. The youngster didn't need to be exposed to the blood.

Kristen flinched but remained silent as he carefully rolled back the sleeve of her ripped sweater, cleaned the cuts, applied antibiotic ointment and taped a sterile pad over them.

"What should I do with this?" Beatrice held up the unfurled blanket.

"Put it over Kristen's shoulders."

The little girl stood and did as he asked.

Clint tucked it around her, his face inches from hers as she shivered again. "This will warm you up fast."

"I'm f-fine."

"Right." He gave her a wry look, then addressed Beatrice. "Did you get the Power-Bar unwrapped?"

"Uh-huh." She gave it to him.

He passed it over to Kristen. "Eat this."

"I'm not hungry."

He leaned close again. "Do you want to walk out of here? Because you're in no condition to do that yet. And you won't be for quite a while unless you eat something and drink this." He pulled a bottle of water out of his backpack, twisted off the cap and set it beside her.

In silence, she took the bar and bit into it.

By the time she finished the bar and half the bottle of water, her shaking had subsided, her color was more normal and her breathing had deepened.

"Better." He studied her, then gentled his voice and touched her cheek, surprised to discover his own fingers were quivering. "You ready to get out of here?"

"Yes." Beatrice answered instead, handing him the wrapper from the chocolate candy bar she'd dug out of the backpack at his direction and quickly devoured.

Kristen managed a smile as she covered his hand with hers where it rested on her cheek. "I am, too."

Her words trembled, but the soft look in her eyes told him shock wasn't the reason for her unsteadiness this time.

He stayed on one knee beside her, fighting the urge to dip his head and claim the kiss he'd been thinking about for weeks. Instead, he settled for a quick brush of his lips over her forehead. That would have to suffice for now—even if her sudden flush tempted him to offer more.

"Wait a second and I'll give you a hand up." He rose, settled his backpack into position on his shoulders and reached down for her. "Take it slow and easy."

He drew her to her feet, watching for any sign of dizziness. But she seemed steady enough as he tucked the blanket more securely around her shoulders.

"I'm okay. I'll make it. But I wouldn't mind holding on to an arm."

"Not a problem." He extended it, and with Beatrice on his other side they circled around the lion and made their way back to the trail. Once there, he paused to mark the spot by tying a strip of yellow plastic around a small seedling. Then, as the fog hovered over them, still cloaking the redwoods in a gray shroud, he led them toward the trailhead.

Much to his relief, Kristen did fine. Though she had to be hurting, she gave no indication of it. Her steps were sure, and she even managed to carry on a sporadic conversation with her daughter.

He was the one who was suddenly overcome by the shakes—inside, at least. Because with every step they took, it became clearer to him how close he'd come to losing her. She might have been able to fight off the mountain lion for a few minutes, and there was a remote chance she'd have driven him away if he wasn't too determined.

But the odds were far greater she'd have ended up dead or badly injured. And Beatrice might have, too.

The churning in his gut intensified, forcing him to acknowledge a truth he'd been dodging for weeks.

Kristen wasn't just starting to make inroads on his heart.

She'd already claimed it.

And as the fog continued to swirl around them, as he worked to keep them on a steady course toward safety, he could only pray that in time she'd come to the same conclusion about him.

"I'll wait in the living room, Kristen. Good night, Beatrice."

"Night, Clint."

"I'll be out in a minute." Kristen smiled over at the man who'd shown up in the nick of time earlier in the evening, spent hours with her in the emergency room, then driven her home, shared a pizza with them and helped her put a very tired little girl to bed.

Although Beatrice had just climbed under the covers, her eyes were already drooping. No wonder. It was close to midnight.

"Good night, honey." She leaned over and kissed her daughter's forehead.

"Aunt Kristen?"

"Mmm-hmm?"

"That mountain lion was really scary today."

"Yes, he was." No sense denying the obvious. But no sense encouraging Beatrice to dwell on it, either. "Everything turned out fine, though, didn't it?"

"Yeah." Beatrice chewed on her lower lip and continued in a smaller voice. "Do you think he would have…eaten us, if Clint hadn't come along?"

"Not if I could help it." Kristen forced her lips into the semblance of a smile. The probability of that scenario was all too real—and still too fresh in her mind. "I used to be a decent softball player, so I know how to swing a bat. He would have gotten a few lumps if he'd tried. Hopefully that would have discouraged him and he'd have run away."

But she doubted it. From what she'd read in the brochures Clint had given her that first day in the visitor center, a mountain lion that got that close wasn't looking to make friends. It was looking for dinner.

"You might have gotten hurt a lot worse trying to protect me, though." Faint creases appeared on Beatrice's brow.

She smoothed the fine hair back from her daughter's forehead. "I wouldn't have cared. I'd do anything to keep anyone or anything from hurting you. And I always will."

Beatrice creased the edge of the blanket between her fingers. "My mom and dad always told me that, too."

"That's because when you love some-one, you care more about them than you do about yourself."

Beatrice's hands stilled. Then one of

them crept toward Kristen and slipped into her grasp. "I care about you, too."

The soft words warmed a cold, empty place deep in Kristen's heart and filled it to overflowing with gratitude. *Thank You, God, for that priceless gift.*

"It makes me happy you feel that way, honey." Clearing the tightness from her throat, she leaned down and once more kissed her daughter. "Now it's long past your bedtime. Go to sleep, okay?"

"Are you going to bed, too?"

"In a little while. I want to talk to Clint first."

Now that her daughter was tucked away for the night, she was looking forward to spending a few minutes with the man who had long ago transitioned from landlord to friend—and was rapidly becoming much more than that. And she was also looking forward to sharing with him some of the insights she'd had during the past few hours.

As she rose to turn out the light, Beatrice yawned and curled up under the covers, her eyes drifting closed. "Would you tell him I care about him, too?"

"I'll do that." Kristen exited into the hall, shutting the door halfway behind her.

Clint was waiting for her with a mug of herbal tea when she reached the dinette table.

"I thought about brewing coffee, but you need to sleep tonight." He smiled as he set the tea on the table and gestured for her to take a seat.

She eyed his mug and sniffed the distinctive aroma of java. "What about you?"

"This is instant. And I don't think I'm going to sleep much, anyway."

"I may not, either—no matter what I drink." She sank into the chair.

"Those pain pills they gave you should take care of any insomnia." He took the seat at right angle to her.

"I don't know if I'll take any. This doesn't hurt that much." She lifted her arm, but a liberal application of white gauze hid the butterfly bandages and the dozen stitches underneath.

"It may, once the feeling starts coming back to that area."

"I'll see." She sipped the soothing tea. "Nice. Thanks."

"You're welcome."

"You know, I keep trying not to think of what would have happened if you hadn't shown up." She wrapped her hands around the mug, letting the warmth chase the chill from her fingers. "But I have a feeling even if I manage to keep that nightmare at bay during the day, it will come back to haunt my sleep."

"It may. If it's any consolation, though, nightmares do fade in time."

She reached over and touched the back of his hand, willing him to see the truth of what she intended to say. "Speaking of nightmares—what happened today should help put yours to rest. You saved my life, and probably Beatrice's. You did what you were trained to do, and you did it fast and accurately without any second-guessing."

"Yeah." A muscle flexed in his jaw. "I've had some of those same thoughts. In hindsight, the whole episode does have a certain redemptive quality. But I'm sorry it came at your expense."

"Honestly? I'm just glad it came." She let her words rest in the air for a moment, wanting him to understand—and accept— that she meant them. "The way I see it, you've been through the fire, and now you've come out the other side, better than before. Maybe that's why this outcome was so different."

One side of his mouth lifted in a half smile. "You're a very insightful woman, Kristen Andrews."

She took a sip of tea, summoning up her courage. He'd given her the perfect opening to discuss the second issue on her mind.

"I have some other insights to share with you, too."

He raised an eyebrow. "Such as?"

She tightened her grip on her mug. "Over the past few hours, I've done a lot of soul-searching. And I realized that even though I have serious issues to deal with, and Beatrice has to be my top priority for the immediate future, I shouldn't let the rest of my life slide. I juggle multiple priorities on the job. There's no reason I can't do that in my personal life."

Leaning closer, she locked gazes with him. "The truth is, you're one of my top priorities—and I don't see any reason to tax your patience. If you still want to see where things between us might lead, I say let's go for it. Because you know what? There's never going to be a perfect time for romance."

A slow smile erased the lingering tension from his face, and he pushed his coffee mug aside. "You won't get any arguments from me. But what about Beatrice? Do you think she'll be okay with this?"

Kristen smiled. "Absolutely. In fact, as I was leaving, she asked me to tell you she cares about you."

"The feeling is mutual."

"I know. That's another reason I feel comfortable moving forward."

"Then I think we need to end the prologue and start chapter one." He stood, drew her to her feet and pulled her into the circle of his arms. "In deference to your injury, I'll try to use some restraint. But I warn you—I've been wanting to do this for a long time. Holding back may be tough."

She lifted her bandaged arm out of the way, resting it against his chest, and stepped close enough to see the smoldering embers in the depths of his eyes. "Don't tax your self-restraint on my account."

The embers ignited. "Okay. But don't say I didn't warn you."

Smoothing her hair back, he cupped her face with his palms. For several long moments he simply gazed down at her, the unbridled tenderness and devotion in his eyes so intense it robbed her legs of their strength.

Fortunately, he was holding her fast in the sheltering circle of his arms. The very place she intended to stay—for always.

When at last he leaned down, she rose on tiptoe, meeting him halfway. And as his lips claimed hers in a kiss filled with longing, love and an ardor that took her breath away, Kristen knew the Orchid Café place mats had it right after all.

Dreams really did come true in Starfish Bay.

Epilogue

Two and a Half Months Later

"This is the best ice-cream social I've ever been to." Chocolate cupcake in one hand, chocolate ice cream in the other, Beatrice beamed up at Kristen, the sparkle on her fairy-princess-painted face glistening in the late-afternoon sun.

"I'm glad to hear that. And everybody else seems to be having fun, too."

She glanced around the open area on The Point where the interpretive trail for the nature preserve began. The entire population of Starfish Bay seemed to have turned out for the event.

Lindsey and Nate, along with Scott, Cindy and Jarrod, were watching the magician perform some up-close magic.

Lindsey's father, Jack, and Scott's mother, Barbara, were having an animated conversation over cupcakes and lemonade at one of the tables the inn had set up. According to Genevieve, Jack had grown partial not only to the killer carrot cake Barbara baked for the Orchid, but to the baker herself. The café owner was all atwitter over that developing senior romance.

Genevieve and Lillian were on hand, of course, licking ice cream cones as they chatted with the mayor and Janice from the art gallery.

Even Jaz had stolen away from his restaurant for a few minutes to enjoy some ice cream.

Everyone was here.

Except Clint.

"What time is Clint coming, Aunt Kristen?"

With a smile at her daughter, she checked

her watch. "You just read my mind. Holiday weekends are busy at the park, but he promised to get here as fast as he could once his shift ended."

"Then he'll be here soon, because he always keeps his promises."

"Yes, he does." As the past few months had confirmed, Clint Nolan was a man of honor and integrity.

And she was head over heels in love with him.

"Aunt Kristen...how am I supposed to eat all this stuff?" Beatrice frowned at her two occupied hands as she puzzled over her dilemma.

"Why don't we go sit by the Watsons? It looks like there are a couple of empty seats at their table."

"Good idea." Beatrice trotted over and plopped down next to Rose. The two girls—now BFFs, according to her daughter—immediately struck up an animated exchange.

"Great party." Ruth smiled and motioned

toward an empty spot on the picnic bench beside her as Kristen approached.

"Indeed it is." Genevieve paused to join the conversation en route to the food table. "Just like old times. Reverend Tobias would be so happy to see the tradition he started being revived. Though I must say the food is better than ever, with the inn sponsoring it. I've already had my ice cream. Now it's on to the cupcakes." She patted her ample waist. "At this rate, I may have to take a hike on Clint's nature trail to burn off all the calories. Where is he, by the way?"

"Working." Kristen's lips twitched as she inspected the woman's flower-bedecked straw hat, which was more suitable for an afternoon tea than an ice-cream social in the woods. "But he'll be here soon."

"He's here now."

At the familiar baritone voice behind her, Kristen turned. He was still wearing his uniform, meaning he'd come directly to the social from work—as promised.

With a flourish, he pulled a pink balloon

that had been twisted into two intertwined hearts from behind his back. "Courtesy of the balloon artist, who was happy to take a special request."

"Now isn't that sweet!" Genevieve sent him a glowing smile. "And so romantic."

He winked at the older woman as he presented the hearts to Kristen. "Wait. There's more." Bending down, he brushed his lips over hers and spoke in a soft voice only she could hear. "I'll do better later."

To hide the warmth that stole onto her cheeks, Kristen leaned over and wiped a smudge of chocolate off the corner of Beatrice's mouth.

"I do believe I'm going to melt into a gooey little puddle right here." Genevieve let out a dramatic sigh. "Wait till I tell Lillian about this. We've been avidly following your romance, you know. And so far, you're getting high marks as a beau. You got bonus points for having us bake that heart-shaped cake on Kristen's birthday last month."

"I liked that, too," Beatrice piped up.

"And the bestest thing was that it was chocolate."

Chuckling, Genevieve patted Beatrice's head. "I agree. Chocolate is hard to beat." With a flutter of fingers, she bustled off in search of Lillian, her cupcake quest forgotten.

"Hi, Clint."

At Beatrice's greeting, he dropped down beside her and pulled another piece of balloon art from behind his back. "I thought you might like this one."

Squealing with delight, she accepted the detailed rendering of Ariel. "Thank you!" She threw her arms around his neck, rewarding him with a hug.

"You're very welcome." He stepped back and examined her painted face. "My goodness, you look magical. May I take your picture?"

"Can Rose be in it with me? She got her face painted, too."

"Of course."

Beatrice took her friend's hand, and

Kristen smiled as the two girls mugged for the photo.

But her smile froze when Beatrice spoke to Ruth as Clint started to slide the camera back into his shirt pocket.

"Would you take a picture of me and Clint and my mom?"

Kristen stopped breathing.

My mom.

Not *my birth mother.*

Beatrice had never referred to her by that title before.

Clint looked over at her, and his slow smile told Kristen he'd caught the significance, too. Beatrice might still call her "Aunt," but in her heart she'd begun to think of her as "Mom."

Perhaps, in time, the title would come, too.

"That's a great idea." Ruth stood and took the camera from Clint. "Now get close together."

The three of them huddled, Beatrice in

the middle. And as the camera clicked, Kristen had just one thought.

Could this day get any better?

Clint polished off his second chocolate cupcake, washed it down with a swig of lemonade and gave Kristen a sheepish grin. "Sorry. I didn't have a chance to eat lunch."

"There's ice cream, too."

"Nope. I'm done." He wiped his lips on a paper napkin, stood and held out his hand. "Want to take a walk?"

"On the nature trail?"

"Why not? Things are starting to wind down here."

She let him pull her to her feet, then surveyed the milling crowd, which was beginning to thin. Clint hoped she'd go along with his idea willingly, but he'd push if he had to. He had plans for this afternoon—and he wasn't going to defer them.

"I don't know…" She bit her lower lip. "Besides, what about Beatrice?"

"Ruth will keep an eye on her. I already asked."

"Is that right?" She planted her hands on her hips. "And when did you manage to arrange that?"

"While you got me the lemonade." He smiled at her. "Pretty please?"

She tried to look stern, but it only made her look cute. "You know I can't resist that dimple of yours."

He gave her an unrepentant grin. "That's what I'm counting on."

Capitulating with a laugh, she gave him a playful nudge with her shoulder. "Okay. Let me do a quick circuit and make sure everything's under control."

"No problem." He lifted his lemonade in salute. "I'm in no hurry. The rest of my day is yours."

"Mmm. Hold that thought."

He sat again, watching her weave through the crowd, an appreciative smile curving his lips. Willowy and lithe, she moved with a quiet, natural grace that reminded him of a ballerina. He'd told her that once, and asked if she'd studied dance. Her response had been a laugh and a claim that she had two left feet.

He didn't believe that.

And he intended to prove that to himself at the first possible opportunity. Swaying with her to a romantic tune was high on his priority list.

He leaned back and took a sip of the fresh-squeezed lemonade, the tart and sweet flavors mingling on his tongue as he followed her progress. She conversed with guests, checked the food supply, exchanged a few words with the inn's catering staff and handed off the balloon hearts to Beatrice for safekeeping—all the while sending him glances that told him she was moving as fast as possible and anxious to rejoin him.

No more anxious than he was to have her by his side.

He set his empty cup on the table, the lingering flavor of the lemonade sweet rather than tart on his tongue. Just like his lingering impression of Kristen. Who could have guessed when she splattered him with mud that first day on The Point—and startled him with her resemblance to Lisa—that she'd end up winning his heart? Certainly not him. He'd planned to walk a wide circle around the new concierge.

Funny how God had had other plans.

As she completed her circuit at last and headed his direction, he rose, giving her an appreciative perusal. He might have been put off by her inappropriate tropical attire when they'd first met, but he'd come to appreciate her excellent taste. Her moss-green capri slacks, short-sleeved fern-patterned sweater and strappy flat sandals were classy and elegant.

Like the lady herself.

"Miss me?" She gave him an impish grin.

He took her hand, glancing down at the twin scars on her forearm—a constant reminder of how close he'd come to losing her. There'd been no complications with rabies or infection, and the angry red marks were beginning to fade, but the memory would take far longer to dim.

His attention still on the scars, he lifted her hand to his lips. "Always."

She swayed toward him as he kissed her fingers, forcing him to shift his attention to the beautiful face that filled his dreams and brightened his days.

"Let's focus on the future, not the past, okay? Everything turned out fine. Better than fine." She slipped her arm through his. "I thought you promised me a walk?"

As usual, she was able to gently tease him out of darkness and into the light.

Yet one more thing he loved about her—and gave thanks for every day.

"I did." He started down the wood-chipped path that wound through the spruce and hemlock trees, toward the sea at The Point. In moments they'd left the crowd behind. "And speaking of things turning out fine, I think you reached a milestone today with Beatrice."

Her features softened. "I know. I guess God finally heard my prayers."

"I'm certain God had a hand in her evolution, but you've done your part to earn that title, too. You're a wonderful mother."

A flush of pleasure suffused her cheeks. "Thank you for saying that. But I still have a lot to learn."

"My mom always claimed motherhood was like running an endless obstacle course. Just when you think you've maneuvered safely through all the hurdles, another one pops up."

"Gee, thanks a lot for the encouragement." She wrinkled her nose at him.

He smiled and laid his hand over the one tucked in his arm. "If you want my opinion, you're doing fine."

They continued in companionable silence until they arrived at the edge of the nature preserve and emerged onto inn property.

"Why don't we sit on the bench for a few minutes?" He gestured toward the chapel.

She hesitated. "I don't want to impose on Ruth for too long."

"I told her we might be gone awhile. She was fine with that."

"In that case…" She smiled and twined her fingers with his. "I'm all yours."

He hoped that was true. Forever.

And he'd soon find out.

His pulse kicked up a notch, and with a squeeze of her fingers, he led her forward. As they rounded the chapel, the silver-wrapped package with the white bow that Lindsey had agreed to deliver came into view.

Beside him, Kristen's step faltered. "There was a wedding here yesterday. Do you suppose someone forgot their present?"

"Let's check it out."

They continued to the bench, and Kristen bent to examine the gift tag. Raising her head, she gave him a surprised look. "For me? From you?"

He smiled. "I don't know anyone else named Kristen."

She examined the shoe-box-sized package. "My birthday was last month."

"This isn't a birthday gift."

"Then what's the occasion?"

"There's only one way to find out." He motioned to the bench. "Why don't we sit while you open it?"

She complied in silence, settling the package in her lap. As he sat beside her, she worked the tape loose, pulled back the wrapping paper and lifted the lid.

Clint's heart began to thump—hard.

She dug through the Styrofoam peanuts with her fingers. Felt around. Froze.

Slanting him a tentative look, she slowly withdrew the small, square ring box.

"Wow." She cradled it in her hand and ran a trembling finger over the velvet top. "Wow."

Gently he took the box from her, his own hands none too steady. "I hope that's a good wow."

"It's a very good wow." Her ebullient expression confirmed her words. "But you fooled me with the big box."

"That was the idea. I didn't want to tip my hand too soon." He flipped up the lid to reveal a large, square-cut diamond set in a gold band.

"Oh!" She breathed rather than said the word as she stared at it. "Triple wow."

He removed the ring and set the box aside, then enfolded her slender fingers in his. She lifted her head to look up at him, and at the love in her luminous green eyes, his heart skipped a beat.

Praying his voice didn't fail him, he launched into the speech he'd been practicing every spare minute for the past ten days—before he fell asleep at night, in the shower, on the trail at the park. He'd even recited it to a banana slug who'd happened along when he'd stopped for lunch beside a downed redwood two days ago.

He hoped Kristen was more responsive than the slug had been.

"I've had that ring since the week after your encounter with the mountain lion. But even before that, I knew you were the woman I wanted to spend the rest of my life with. Given all you have on your plate, though, I didn't want to rush you. I figured you needed more time to be certain. So I've tried to move slowly. However, my patience ran out a few days ago."

He stroked his thumb over the back of her hand. "I said earlier that the rest of my day is yours. The truth is, the rest of my *life* is yours, if you'll have me. But if you're not ready to hear that, I'm prepared to put this ring away and try again down the road."

"No." She placed her free hand over his, her tone firm—and confident. "I'm more than ready. I've known for months, too. And I've prayed about it." She looked up, tracing the length of the tall white steeple on Starfish Bay Chapel. "I've bent the Lord's ear more in the past few months than I have in the past ten years, and the truth is, being with you feels right in here." She tapped her heart.

"It feels right to me, too." He lifted the ring, and the facets sparkled in the setting sun. "When we met here on The Point a few months ago, I never expected to fall in love with you. But the more time we've

spent together, the more I began to realize how special you are. You're strong and
smart and caring and kind. You surprise
me and make me laugh and fill my life
with joy in a way no one—no one, Kristen—" he emphasized that point to ensure
she got the message "—ever has. Even on
cloudy days, you make the sun shine in
my heart."

His voice hoarsened, and he cleared his
throat as he lifted her left hand. "Kristen
Andrews, I love you more than words can
express. And I promise to honor and cher-
ish you all the days of my life. So without
any more speeches—would you do me the
honor of becoming my wife?"

The radiance in her face put the luster of
the diamond in his fingers to shame as she
whispered her response. "Yes."

Joy spilled over in his heart, and he
slipped the ring on her slender finger, seal-
ing their engagement with a visible symbol
of the love and fidelity they would soon
declare before God.

The sooner the better, as far as he was concerned.

As if reading his mind, Kristen smiled up at him. "What would you think about a Thanksgiving wedding here, in Starfish Bay Chapel? I can get us a great deal. I have connections."

The corners of his lips twitched. "I knew there was a reason I fell in love with a concierge."

She scooted closer and put her arms around his neck. "Oh, I have access to all kinds of perks. For example, Mattson has resorts in some great honeymoon destinations."

"I like the sound of that. But let's make a deal. You plan the wedding—I'll plan the honeymoon. And I promise you a memorable one."

Her eyes twinkled. "I have no doubt of that."

"In the meantime, though..." He touched his forehead to hers, their lips a whisper apart. "I think we have an engagement to celebrate."

"Mmm." She exhaled, her breath warm on his cheek. "Did you have something specific in mind?"

"Oh, yeah." He eased back a few inches to see her face. "If I could have arranged it, I'd have brought in a marching band and organized a fireworks display and taken out a full-page ad in every newspaper in the country announcing that the most wonderful woman in the world has agreed to be my wife. That not being possible, I've booked a table at the swankiest restaurant in Eureka."

Eyes glistening, she touched his cheek and whispered the most beautiful words he'd ever heard. "I love you, Clint Nolan."

He gazed at her radiant face, drinking in every nuance of her tender expression. Wishing this moment could last forever. And knowing that for as long as he lived, it would shine in his memory as brilliantly as the diamond glinting on her finger.

"As for celebrations, why don't we start with this?" She linked her arms around his neck and gently pulled him toward her.

He didn't resist.

This was where they belonged. Together, for always.

And as their lips touched...joined... melded in a kiss filled with promise, passion and hope, he gave thanks.

For second chances.

For unexpected blessings.

And for happy endings.

* * * * *

Dear Reader,

If you've dropped into Starfish Bay for the first time—welcome! For those of you who are returning after previous visits in *Seaside Reunion* and *Finding Home,* I'm delighted you've come back.

I saved a special story for last. Clint Nolan's made appearances here and there since the beginning of the series, sort of a mysterious but intriguing presence. In this book, his secrets are revealed, thanks to the charming concierge at the new inn who infiltrates his heart…and has secrets of her own. From day one, it does *not* appear to be a match made in heaven. But sometimes God surprises us with His plans.

I hope you savor this final visit to Starfish Bay, a place that has become as real to me as any actual town on the beautiful Northern California coast. While it's always hard to say goodbye, it's also fun to move on to the next adventure.

Please check my website at www.irenehannon.com for more information about my other books. And do join me soon for another captivating and heartwarming romance!

Irene Hannon

Questions for Discussion

1. First impressions are important—and negative ones are sometimes difficult to overcome. Clint and Kristen get off to a rocky start. Choose three words to describe how each viewed the other after that initial encounter.

2. Have you ever met someone who looked like a person you didn't like—or shared his or her name? Did it influence your impression of that person? If so, in what way?

3. Kristen is a bit put off by Jaz and his restaurant, yet neither turns out to be what she expects. What is the danger of forming an impression based on appearance?

4. Both Kristen and Clint are dealing with traumatic events in their pasts that have left them with a legacy of guilt.

Do you think that guilt is justified for either character? Why or why not?

5. Kristen has lost touch with God, believing she's not worthy of forgiveness. How might you counsel her to reestablish that relationship?

6. Do you think the characters in this book grew during the course of the story? How? Cite some specific examples to support your opinion.

7. When Kristen inherits the grief-stricken Beatrice, she has no idea how to deal with her. What advice would you have offered?

8. At one point, Clint admits that, in hindsight, he and his former fiancée may not have been the best match. He cites their different interests and priorities. How important is it in a relationship for two people to share these things? What problems might arise if they don't?

9. From the beginning, Clint connects with Beatrice. What does he do to win the little girl's trust and affection?

10. Both Kristen and Clint cite pride as one of the reasons for their mistakes. What does the Bible say about pride? What are some of the dangers of pride?

11. What is the one thing you will most remember about this book? Why?

REQUEST YOUR FREE BOOKS!

2 FREE INSPIRATIONAL NOVELS IN TRUE LARGE PRINT
PLUS 2 FREE MYSTERY GIFTS

Love Inspired
TRUE LARGE PRINT

YES! Please send me 2 FREE Love Inspired® True Large Print novels and my 2 FREE mystery gifts (gifts are worth about $10). After receiving them, if I don't wish to receive any more books, I can return the shipping statement marked "cancel." If I don't cancel, I will receive 3 brand-new true large print novels every month and be billed just $7.99 per book in the U.S. or $9.99 per book in Canada. That's a savings of at least 20% off the cover price. It's quite a bargain! Shipping and handling is just 50¢ per book in the U.S. and 75¢ per book in Canada.* I understand that accepting the 2 free books and gifts places me under no obligation to buy anything. I can always return the shipment and cancel at any time. Even if I never buy another book, the two free books and gifts are mine to keep forever.

117/317 IDN F5FZ

Name _____ (PLEASE PRINT) _____

Address _____ Apt. # _____

City _____ State/Prov. _____ Zip/Postal Code _____

Signature (if under 18, a parent or guardian must sign) _____

Mail to the Harlequin® Reader Service:
IN U.S.A.: P.O. Box 1867, Buffalo, NY 14240-1867
IN CANADA: P.O. Box 609, Fort Erie, Ontario L2A 5X3

* Terms and prices subject to change without notice. Prices do not include applicable taxes. Sales tax applicable in N.Y. Canadian residents will be charged applicable taxes. Offer not valid in Quebec. This offer is limited to one order per household. Not valid for current subscribers to Love Inspired True Large Print books. All orders subject to credit approval. Credit or debit balances in a customer's account(s) may be offset by any other outstanding balance owed by or to the customer. Please allow 4 to 6 weeks for delivery. Offer available while quantities last.

Your Privacy—The Harlequin® Reader Service is committed to protecting your privacy. Our Privacy Policy is available online at www.ReaderService.com or upon request from the Harlequin Reader Service.

We make a portion of our mailing list available to reputable third parties that offer products we believe may interest you. If you prefer that we not exchange your name with third parties, or if you wish to clarify or modify your communication preferences, please visit us at www.ReaderService.com/consumerschoice or write to us at Harlequin Reader Service Preference Service, P.O. Box 9062, Buffalo, NY 14269. Include your complete name and address.

REQUEST YOUR FREE BOOKS!
2 FREE RIVETING INSPIRATIONAL NOVELS IN TRUE LARGE PRINT PLUS 2 FREE MYSTERY GIFTS

Love Inspired®
SUSPENSE

TRUE LARGE PRINT

YES! Please send me 2 FREE Love Inspired® Suspense True Large Print novels and my 2 FREE mystery gifts (gifts are worth about $10). After receiving them, if I don't wish to receive any more books, I can return the shipping statement marked "cancel." If I don't cancel, I will receive 3 brand-new true large print novels every month and be billed just $7.99 per book in the U.S. or $9.99 per book in Canada. That's a savings of at least 20% off the cover price. It's quite a bargain! Shipping and handling is just 50¢ per book in the U.S. and 75¢ per book in Canada.* I understand that accepting the 2 free books and gifts places me under no obligation to buy anything. I can always return the shipment and cancel at any time. Even if I never buy another book, the two free books and gifts are mine to keep forever.

124/324 IDN F5GD

Name	(PLEASE PRINT)

Address	Apt. #

City	State/Prov.	Zip/Postal Code

Signature (if under 18, a parent or guardian must sign)

Mail to the Harlequin® Reader Service:
IN U.S.A.: P.O. Box 1867, Buffalo, NY 14240-1867
IN CANADA: P.O. Box 609, Fort Erie, Ontario L2A 5X3

* Terms and prices subject to change without notice. Prices do not include applicable taxes. Sales tax applicable in N.Y. Canadian residents will be charged applicable taxes. Offer not valid in Quebec. This offer is limited to one order per household. Not valid for current subscribers to Love Inspired Suspense True Large Print books. All orders subject to credit approval. Credit or debit balances in a customer's account(s) may be offset by any other outstanding balance owed by or to the customer. Please allow 4 to 6 weeks for delivery. Offer available while quantities last.

Your Privacy—The Harlequin® Reader Service is committed to protecting your privacy. Our Privacy Policy is available online at www.ReaderService.com or upon request from the Harlequin Reader Service.

We make a portion of our mailing list available to reputable third parties that offer products we believe may interest you. If you prefer that we not exchange your name with third parties, or if you wish to clarify or modify your communication preferences, please visit us at www.ReaderService.com/consumerschoice or write to us at Harlequin Reader Service Preference Service, P.O. Box 9062, Buffalo, NY 14269. Include your complete name and address.

LISTLP13TRR